SHADOW DAYS

Cedar Hollow Series, Book 4

by

Melinda Clayton

Thomas-Jacob Publishing, LLC
USA

SHADOW DAYS

by Melinda Clayton

Copyright 2014 Melinda Clayton

Published by: Thomas-Jacob Publishing, LLC
ThomasJacobPublishing@gmail.com

This book is a work of fiction. While some of the places referenced may be real, characters and incidents are the product of the author's imagination and are used fictitiously. Any resemblance to events or persons living or dead is purely coincidental.

Cover Typeface (Title): *Boycott.ttf*, from Flat-it, http://flat-it.com, under the End Users License Agreement (EULA) for free fonts.

Cover Typeface (Subtitle): *DejaVu Serif*, from FontSquirrel, http://www.fontsquirrel.com/fonts/dejavu-serif, under the DejaVu Fonts License v1.00.

Symbol Typeface (short story): Nymphette Font, created by Nymphont. Available from http://www.fontspace.com/nymphont/nymphette under a Commercial Use Freeward License.

ISBN-13: 978-0-9895729-6-5

ISBN-10: 0-9895729-6-X

WorldCat OCLC Control Number: 933288775

First Edition

First Printing: November 2014

Printed in the United States of America

Dedication

To all who have come to love Cedar Hollow and its residents, I thank you. Writing this book felt, in many ways, like coming home.

With a special thank you to W. Michael Franklin, for allowing me to build upon the character of Sheriff John Moore. Sheriff Moore's character was originally developed in Mr. Franklin's short story, *The Sheriff of Cedar Hollow*.

Acknowledgments

Many thanks to my editor, Smoky Zeidel, and to my beta-readers: Jim Bessey, Kae Bender, and Bill and Patty Franklin. I couldn't have done it without you. Any leftover mistakes are solely my own.

My days are like a long shadow. I have withered like grass.

~ Psalm 102:11

Chapter 1: Emily Holt

I don't think it's too much of an exaggeration to say I lost my mind in the early morning hours of April 18, 2015. I wasn't sorry to see it go; it had been fighting to get away from me for the better part of a decade, and I was exhausted. Besides, I figured it was finally my turn.

I'd felt for years as if my mind were shrinking, slowly shriveling up and crumbling away. It was a sneaky process, but I knew. I'd once prided myself on my ability to hold my own during a conversation, whether it was about global subjects such as religion and politics, or more local matters such as who'd just been laid off and which farmers' market offered the best tomatoes. But more and more often over the years, I'd found myself losing my train of thought halfway into a comment, or I'd call one neighbor by another neighbor's name.

It bothered me, this encroaching mental dullness; it angered me, too. I'd been angry for years. I couldn't help feeling as if the fact I'd spent so many years maintaining sanity for two was to blame. After all, to my way of thinking, that divided my own in half. It's difficult enough to navigate through life maintaining one's own sanity; just imagine having to maintain someone else's as well.

True, I'd never been a certified genius, and I'd always had a bit of flightiness, but I'd been sharp enough that the numbers representing my IQ score had always managed to hover close to those signifying my weight, and that's saying something the last few years. I was relatively certain that was no longer the case, though, and not just because I'd put on a few pounds. Yes, I was angry.

Hold it together. That was the crux of it all, really. It's an interesting turn of phrase, isn't it? It conjures up all sorts of visual imagery. I have a ridiculous mental picture of me, dressed in my usual attire of flip-flops and mommy jeans, standing face to the wind on an unnamed cliff somewhere, cartoon arms stretched enormously long to encircle my home and family. There I am, *holding it together* against...what? Life? What an absurd idea. If my experience is anything to go by, that's an absolutely pointless battle. There's no winning against Life. That bastard'll run you right over and laugh on his way out the door.

These thoughts weren't something I'd mentioned to anyone close to me, possibly—probably—because there *wasn't* anyone close to me. My children, who no doubt loved me, were nearly grown, both in college and focused not on the messy past they'd left behind, but on the shiny futures their expensive educations were supposed to ensure. I had no close friends; it's difficult to maintain friendships when your whole life is about keeping a secret. And my husband, God rest his soul, was dead. Greg had died unexpectedly exactly one year prior to the humid spring morning on which I lost my mind.

There are those who no doubt believe my husband's passing caused the unraveling of my sanity, and in some ways, they're probably right. Just not in the ways they think. Not even my children know all the facts behind Greg's death, or his life either, for that matter. Far from it. Some days I think I should tell them, other days I know to leave well enough alone.

All that aside, I must say it was liberating to let go of everything, positively invigorating, to tell the truth. Who knew it could feel so glorious? Well, I suppose Greg had known, but he'd kept that secret to himself, and if you think *that* didn't help stoke my anger ... well. At any rate, when my mind finally let go, it snapped so loudly I could hear it. It sounded like freedom.

I'd been lying in bed as I had for months, since just after Greg died. I could see the future stretching ahead of me, and it looked exactly like the past year. I'd grow older, of course, but nothing would change. I'd continue to miss my kids and they'd continue to move both farther and further away from me, exactly as they'd done since the day they were born. I'd call them; they'd return my calls out of a sense of obligation. I'd continue to buy groceries on Fridays, do yard work on Saturdays, and clean house on Sundays, and I'd still run out of cereal, the weeds would return with a vengeance, and mildew would reclaim the tiles. I couldn't stand it, could not *stand* it, I tell you, could not *bear* seeing that endless tunnel of sameness. And then … *snap*. The weight was gone.

Poof.

I literally jumped out of bed and threw on the first clothes I could find: a pair of shapeless grey sweatpants my children despised and a brown plaid cotton blouse my husband had hated. Both made me laugh, not a sane laugh, I'm sure, but a good one. Then I dug through the closet, throwing shoes and boxes and blankets aside until I found exactly what I was looking for: red leather cowgirl boots bought on a whim eons ago, back when I was young enough to think of life in terms of *someday* instead of *too late*.

A hat, I told myself. That had been one of the *somedays*. *Someday I'll buy a hat*. Then and there, I promised myself I'd buy a hat at the earliest opportunity, a cowgirl hat, red, to match my boots. The fact that sweatpants and cowgirl boots don't typically go together didn't bother me in the least, but I wasn't exactly firing on all cylinders, as my late husband would have said.

Sometimes I don't think I'm firing on all cylinders, Emily. The memory surfaced unbidden, and I smacked it away. *No shit, Sherlock.* Not the nicest mental response to my husband's ghost, but the best I could manage at that moment. I shoved the spilled blankets and shoes back into my closet and knelt on the floor to survey my boots. I wasn't even sure they'd still fit; I couldn't remember the last time I'd worn them. I thought it was probably the last time I'd gone dancing, which would have been before the kids were born. I was sure it was before I could feel my belly pushing against my thighs as I knelt on the floor.

Once upon a time, long, long ago, I had been a woman of style, though that may be hard to fathom given the choices I made that morning. But it's true; style had been my profession, and even as I squeezed my calves into those boots, I somehow knew the remnants of my old career were still lurking inside of me, just waiting to be released. They wouldn't, however, be released that morning. I haphazardly threw some clothes into a suitcase, neither noticing nor caring what they were or how they landed.

Finally, I picked up my purse, fished out my car keys and left, backing out of the garage into the soggy dawn, steering carefully down the drive without bothering to set the alarm or lock the gate.

For the first time in over forty years I didn't even make my bed; I was that rebellious. I cranked up the radio, searching between stations before settling on Billy Joel's *My Life*. That's right, I said loudly to absolutely no one. It's my life. Leave me alone. Leave me the ... phooey. I couldn't quite bring myself to say *that* word yet; you know the one. But the sentiment was there.

I had no idea where I was going, but I headed north. With a starting location of Jacksonville, Florida, north seemed full of possibilities. I'd drive to the end of the road, and then ... Well, that remained to be seen. And that was precisely the point.

Chapter 2: Emily Holt

As it happened, the end of the road was somewhere just south of Huntington, West Virginia. That wasn't what I'd been expecting, but I'd begun to understand my expectations were often a deficit, one of those traps I never knew I was setting for myself until I'd fallen into it again. Things always had a way of sounding so much more exciting than they turned out to be. For instance, who would have ever thought the end of the road would be a hairpin curve in the middle of nowhere?

Such were my thoughts that chilly afternoon when my car gave a final sigh and coasted to a stop on the side of a meandering county road heading, best I could tell, slightly west. I'd taken I-77 almost to Charlotte before becoming bored with interstate monotony, deciding then to switch to the John Steinbeck approach to travel, roughing it on the back roads, seeing the real America. I'd wound along back roads for days, nearly all the way to Huntington, when my car apparently decided it was time for a nap. The only thing that would make it more *real America*, I figured, struggling to get the car out of the middle of the road before it completely ran out of steam, would be the bill I received once whatever was broken got fixed.

I twisted around, craning my neck to survey the area. There wasn't even room to pull the car entirely off the road. As it was, the passenger side hugged the mountain so closely the mirror nearly touched the rock wall, while the driver's side still jutted a foot into the traffic lane. The other side of the road offered even less in the way of protection; no more than five feet past the asphalt the ground dropped away so steeply my head was even with the treetops. The way I saw it, my options were to stay in the car and be smashed by rocks tumbling down the mountainside, or dare to open my car door and be smashed by cars whizzing around the sharp curve. Neither choice inspired much hope.

Why couldn't I have broken down in Savannah, I wondered, or Gatlinburg? Somewhere touristy, with emergency lanes and parking lots. Why couldn't I have broken down in Asheville? I'd stopped in all of those places along the way, even spending several nights in Asheville. I'd managed to snag a little cabin within walking distance of the Nantahala River, briefly toying with the idea of taking one of those rafting trips, but the water was so cold I'd changed my mind.

I should have done it, I told myself sitting there in the middle of nowhere. I should have just stayed right there. I could have afforded to. Greg had provided well for me; his insurance policies totaled in the seven-figure range.

In the beginning, I'd tried to give away the money. I wanted nothing to do with it. Goodwill, The Salvation Army, the Humane Society, it didn't matter. It felt like blood money to me and I wanted it gone. But the boys had talked me into keeping it, investing some, living off the rest. "It's tough out there, Mom," Zachary had said. "You haven't held a job outside the home in years. You need to keep this. You earned it taking care of all of us. It's what Dad would have wanted."

I'd disagreed with his assessment of what his dad would have wanted, but I sure as hell agreed I'd earned it. I didn't share that news with Zach, of course. It was easier to cave to his wishes than it would have been to break his heart.

Anyway, there I was, stranded on the side of the road when I could have gone rafting instead. I'd always wanted to go whitewater rafting. At least I'd always told myself I did. I wasn't a strong swimmer and I had no idea how to steer a raft, but it was one of those "bucket list" things I'd always said I should do. That, along with skydiving and paragliding and any number of things we're supposed to want to do. For a season or two, the bucket list conversation had been *the* topic at social gatherings, thanks to a blockbuster movie of the same name.

I'd never been brave enough during those conversations to say, "Well, what I'd really like to do is buy a cowgirl hat," so I'd agreed with everyone else that climbing Mount Everest and hiking the Appalachian Trail were things one simply must do before kicking that proverbial bucket. But I'd always left those conversations wondering how many of us were lying through our teeth. I certainly was. I liked the idea of doing all those things, but somewhere along the line I'd figured out the idea often didn't match up to the reality—that expectations thing biting me in the behind again. Besides, given enough time and money, the big things on the list, things like *Live in a Monastery for A Week* and *Go on Safari in Africa*, seemed easier to me to complete than the little things, things like *Wear a Beret to the PTA Meeting* and *Stand Up to Your Mother-in-Law*. Or *Tell Your Children the Truth*. That one was especially hard.

I had always been that way, reluctant to assert myself and then resentful when no one knew what I wanted. It was a stupid way to live, thoroughly unfair to everyone around me. Unfortunately, I hadn't recognized the pattern until Greg brought it to my attention approximately twenty-three-point-six minutes before his car crashed through a guardrail and did a nosedive into the St. Johns River.

We'd been arguing—fighting, actually. I'd gone into the fight with a sense of self-righteous entitlement, and emerged from the other end with a harsh reality check and a dead husband.

Whose fault do you think that is, Emily? Think about it, why don't you? I could still hear his voice, his angry words. *I have, Greg,* I answered him for the millionth time in my head. *I think about it all the time. What do you think set me on the road to Crazyville? How's it feel to share it with me, big boy?*

Memories of Greg were a threat to my insanity, which I happened to be enjoying, so I shook them away and reached for my cell. Reception had been spotty off and on throughout the trip and now, as I sat encased by rock walls, it was non-existent; the bars flatlined across the screen. Taking a deep breath, I reached for the door handle. My plan, such as it was, was to open the door barely a crack and throw myself out and to the left, scrambling around the back of the car before becoming the human equivalent of a squashed bug against the grill of the next vehicle rounding the curve.

What I'd failed to take into consideration was the fact that in my current physical shape and state of dress (the brown plaid had by then been switched out with purple rayon, but the sweatpants and boots had become a staple), squeezing through a cracked door and nimbly throwing myself to safety just wasn't in the cards. To this day I don't know if it was because my boot heel got stuck under the gas pedal, my sleeve got caught on the gearshift, or my hip got caught under the steering wheel, but for whatever reason I ended up hanging half-in and half-out the car door, my head dangling over the pavement, hair swinging along the ground.

Just then I heard the blip of a siren, followed shortly thereafter by the sound of shoes crunching on gravel until a matching set of huge, glossy black oxfords parked themselves right under my nose. I could see my distorted face reflected in the shine.

"Ma'am?" The voice was deep and decidedly puzzled. "Are you okay?"

My right arm was still being held prisoner by my sleeve's relationship with the gearshift, which neither seemed to want to end anytime soon, but luckily for me, my left arm was free, dangling to the side of my head, hand resting in a puddle of mud. I summoned my cheeriest voice and managed to raise my arm just enough to offer the man a jaunty thumbs-up, inadvertently slinging a blob of mud across his pant leg in the process.

"Fine," I chirped. "A-okay, in fact. Just looking for my contact." That's when I started laughing. I laughed until tears formed and rolled across my forehead, landing on the man's shiny shoes. I laughed until I couldn't breathe, until my limbs turned to putty and the car finally released its hold, depositing me at the man's feet like a lump of beached jellyfish.

And still, I laughed.

Chapter 3: Kay Langley

"Oh, my. Looks like someone broke down." Valerie Poindexter, the town's librarian, pointed through the plate glass window of my diner. "Clifford and Maxwell just went by in the truck."

Clifford and Maxwell Hager own Johnson's Repair Shoppe, Cedar Hollow's only option for repair work. It don't matter if it's a car, a washing machine, or a tiller, if it needs fixing, the Hager brothers fix it. They've even been known to fix my grill a time or two when my son, Andrew, can't figure out the problem.

Andrew does the cooking at Peggy's Diner, the little restaurant built by my granddaddy and named for my mother. We're the only diner around for fifty miles, but we have the best food in all of West Virginia, if I do say so myself. We still use my momma's old recipes, although I do have to fuss at Andrew from time to time for trying to get too creative with the spices.

Anyway, the *Johnson's* in the name of the repair shop came from the original owner, John Paul Johnson. When he passed away in 2002, the Hagers bought the place from his widow, Corinne. They left everything exactly the same except for adding an extra *pe* to the word *Shoppe*. "That's how they spell it in the city," Clifford had explained. "It'll class the place up."

I didn't have the heart to tell him I'd only seen that spelling on ice cream parlors and dress shops. In my opinion, it looked a little silly on a repair shop sign, but if a couple of extra letters made him happy, so be it.

I refilled Valerie's tea glass and leaned across the counter to peer out the window. "Someone local?"

Valerie shook her head. "I didn't recognize the car. Toyota, older model. Didn't look wrecked, so that's good, anyway."

"Lucky for them they broke down near here," I said. "Next option would've been Huntington, and you know how that is. They'd be sittin' on the side of the road waitin' on a tow, and payin' twice as much to get it. Must've been where they was headed, though."

Cedar Hollow, population 219, is quite a ways off the main road. Aside from the little train station on the edge of town, we don't get much through traffic; you have to be searching for us in order to find us. Every now and then someone'll pull up to Mr. Smith's General Store for gas, on account of the sign Dennis Lane put up along the highway. If they ain't in too big a hurry they might stop in for a bite to eat before continuing on their way, but that's about all we get as far as outside traffic. All in all, we're a pretty self-contained little town. Seeing a strange car towed back to the repair shop in the early evening hours was bound to draw attention; I was starting to wish I hadn't told Riva to take the afternoon off.

Back in my day, Riva was called our waitress, but times have changed. Going by the new lingo, I suppose Riva would be known as our combination hostess, server, and manager. I've known Riva nearly all my life and love her dearly, but lately she'd taken to nagging me about updating the place. "Kay," she said to me, "this diner has looked the same since I sat at the bar in saddle shoes and bobbysocks with Harold Pritchett and ordered a milkshake from your momma."

I'd initially refused to even consider changing it up, but once I thought about it, I'd been forced to admit things had been kept pretty much the same since my momma added new curtains sometime back in the sixties. I reckon I'd gotten so used to the way it looked I hadn't noticed how faded and worn everything had become. That, and I suppose it's possible a part of me wanted to keep it the way momma had had it; I do miss her, even still. At any rate, I'd finally given in and told Riva if she could find some new curtains that were better than the old, I'd be happy to hang them. I hardly had the words out of my mouth before she'd taken off for Huntington, headed, I suspect, for the mall.

I was happy to give Riva time off; I know she loves that mall. But seeing the Hagers drive by towing a strange car was making me regret my decision. Out-of-the-ordinary happenings in Cedar Hollow always bring people to my diner to speculate on what might be going on. I had a feeling we were about to get busy right when Andrew and I needed to be closing up. Sure enough, the bell above the door started jingling, and I looked over to see Virgil Young, the van driver for the children's lodge Jessie McIntosh had built up on Crutcher Mountain.

"Evenin', ladies," he said, removing his hat and hanging it on one of the hooks inside the door. "Looks like we got a little excitement goin' on."

"We just saw the Hagers go by towing a car," said Valerie. "Who is it, do you know?"

"A woman," said Virgil, settling himself on a stool at the bar. I was already pulling a slice of key lime pie from the cooler. When for generations your family has owned the only diner for fifty miles, you know things, and I knew Virgil Young wanted a piece of my pie with a side of milk. People develop habits and ways of behaving, and Virgil's habit was to stop by my diner in the evening for a piece of pie. Virgil's wife, Mary, is taking cancer treatments. The outlook is good, but it's taken its toll on her and she spends a great deal of the day sleeping. I suspect Virgil's daily visits to my diner are as much about needing company as they are about my pie, but he never says, and I don't ask.

"Well, is she all right?" I asked, pushing a frosty glass over to him.

"Now, that I can't say for sure," he answered around a bite of pie. "When I come 'round the curve Sheriff Moore was pickin' her up off the road. Couldn't tell if she was laughin' or cryin', but she looked to be havin' a hard time standin' up."

Valerie and I exchanged a look, and I knew she was as puzzled as I was. "Pickin' her up off the road?" I asked. "What was she doin' on the road? Was she hurt?" After a moment's reflection, I added, "Was she a Pritchett?"

The Pritchetts have been making, using, and abusing moonshine for decades just outside Cedar Hollow. Most of them are gone now, except for Geraldine, and she's left all that behind. Still, when you hear of a person lolling around in the road laughing, crying, and having trouble standing up, it's hard not to think of the Pritchetts.

Virgil shrugged. "Couldn't say if she was hurt or not. I was goin' to pull over to see if they needed help but the sheriff waved me on by. Wasn't a Pritchett, though, least not a local one. Tags was from Florida."

Before I could think of anything to say to that, the bell announced another visitor, this time my fourteen-year-old granddaughter, Hannah. "Hi, Grandma," she said, "and hi, Dad!" she raised her voice to yell toward the kitchen, where Andrew was taking inventory in the freezer. The dinner special that afternoon had been my momma's chicken and dumplings, and we'd had so many orders Andrew was afraid we'd run out of chicken before the next delivery.

"The sheriff brought some crazy lady to Mr. Smith's General Store," Hannah announced as she helped herself to a piece of chocolate pie from the cooler.

"Hannah!" I said, frowning at her choice of words. "Why would you say a thing like that?"

"Yes, why would you?" asked Valerie, patting the stool beside her, inviting Hannah to sit. "Who was she? What was she doing? Was it the woman with the car?"

"Lord have mercy, Valerie. You're worse than Hannah." I gave her a stern look before turning back to my granddaughter. "But what about it, Hannah? Who was she?"

"I don't know who she was." She paused for a second to lick a speck of chocolate off her thumb. "But she was laughing at nothing. *Nothing.* She'd quit for a minute and then start right back in. Sheriff Moore had to hold her up, and he kept trying to ask her what she needed for the night, but every time she started to answer him she'd just start laughing again. And what she was *wearing*. God, Grandma, if you ever dressed like that I'd disown you."

"Why, Hannah May," I managed to say, before Valerie cut me off again.

"What was she wearing?"

I swear, Valerie was starting to remind me of one of them little yappy dogs, the kind all them Hollywood girls like to carry around tucked up under their arm.

"To start with, some kind of purple shirt." I glanced down at my own purple shirt, ready to defend my choice of clothing, but Hannah kept right on going. "And sweatpants, you know, those ugly grey ones? All stretched out and baggy. Covered with mud, too. And get this." Valerie leaned even closer to Hannah, apparently thinking she might miss something, although I don't see how she could've, seeing as how she was nearly in Hannah's lap. "Red cowgirl boots. Doesn't that sound awful?"

"Sounds to me like somethin' Valerie would have worn back in the day," I said, and sidestepped a swat. Valerie had first come to town back in the seventies, a right cute girl, working in our library to satisfy credits for her degree from Marshall University. But her style had been something else, I'll tell you. Why, she'd been our local hippy. "Remember those beads you used to braid in your hair, Valerie? And that skirt? The one with the colors splashed all over it? What'd you call it?"

"Tie-dyed," she answered drily. "And I'll have you know it was all the rage back then. I was stylish beyond my time. Or at least beyond this town."

"Valerie was the reason half the boys in town started readin'," said Virgil, and unlike me, he wasn't quick enough to dodge Valerie's smack on the arm.

"Anyway," said Valerie, directing her gaze at Hannah, "what's the sheriff going to do with her?"

"I don't know," answered Hannah. "When I left he was trying to pull her up off the floor again, but she was laughing too hard to get up. Kept asking if they had any red cowgirl hats. Why in the world would Mr. Dennis carry red cowgirl hats? And an even better question: Why would anyone want one? Wait." She peered at Valerie. "You wore beads in your hair? Cool. Could you show me how to do that?"

"I'd love to," answered Valerie, shooting me a look I knew was the equivalent of *so there*. I just ignored her. There ain't no winning with Valerie Poindexter.

"My goodness," I said to Hannah. "What about Dennis? Was he able to help?" Dennis Lane is the owner of the grocery. He runs it along with his father, Darryl. Yes, I realize Hannah said the name of the grocery was *Mr. Smith's* and not *Mr. Lane's*, but sort of like with the machine shop, the Lane's left the name of the original owner just as it had always been. Mr. Smith passed away back in the seventies, and after that Billy May Platte owned the store until she passed just a couple of years ago. Then her daughter, Jessie McIntosh—yes, that would be the same one who owns the children's lodge—kept it for a little while before selling it to Dennis Lane. Through all of it, it's always just stayed Mr. Smith's General Store.

Is it any wonder I'm so stuck against changing the diner? Nothing in this town ever changes, and why should it? If it ain't broke, don't fix it, as my daddy used to say. Start calling Mr. Smith's *Mr. Lane's*, and folks won't know what in the world you're talking about.

"Mr. Dennis was trying to grab hold of one of her arms to help her up." Hannah was still telling her story. "Poor old Mr. Lane was just standing there behind the counter with his oxygen tank, saying, 'Well I done seen ever'thin', now. Now I done seen *ever*'thin'.'"

I had to laugh at her perfect impression of Darryl Lane. Darryl, bless his heart, has always been a worrier; I could only imagine what he thought of the shenanigans going on in his son's store. Before we could ask any more questions, the bell jingled again and we looked up to see Sheriff Moore, although had anyone ever told me he'd show up at my diner looking the way he did, I wouldn't have believed it.

Sheriff Moore is always dressed to the nines. Until then, I'd never seen him with a button undone, a hair of his military cut out of place, or a smudge of dirt on one of his spit-shined shoes. Nor had I ever seen him with any expression other than pure business. Our sheriff is a smart man; he does a good job keeping tabs on our little town, but he stays to himself. Not a one of us knows a thing about him outside of his job.

There ain't a woman in town, regardless of her age, who don't primp a little when she sees him coming. He's a handsome one, no doubt, tall and strong and jam-packed with muscle, but he never even seems to notice the looks sneaking his way. Oh, he's polite enough, but he don't ever say much. Stops in for coffee most days, but sits by himself at a corner table and don't mingle with the rest of us.

That day, though, he looked like he'd been through the wringer. His shirt was halfway untucked and his hat was crushed flat with a boot print plain as day stamped across the top of it. His shoes were smudged with dirt and the knees of his pants looked like he'd been kneeling in mud, but out of all that, it was his face that made the biggest impression on me. The man looked shocked out of his senses. Shocked, and plumb wore out.

"Sheriff? You okay?" I reached across the counter toward him, but I wouldn't have touched him. He was not a man who invited touching.

"Coffee," he said, tossing his filthy hat on a hook and taking a seat, not in the corner, for once, but right between Valerie and Virgil. "I'll take some coffee, if you don't mind."

"Of course," I said, starting a fresh pot.

"Better make it a double," he said, rubbing his hand across his face with a sigh. "I know it's late for coffee, but after a day like today I need something, and although I'm off duty, I'm not much of a drinker."

Until then, I'd never heard the sheriff string so many words together at once, so I took my chances. "Sheriff,' I said, "if you don't mind me askin', what did you do with her?"

He didn't even pretend not to know who I meant. "Dropped her off at Vines and Roses," he said, pulling the sugar canister close as if to guard it until his coffee came. "Didn't know what else to do."

"Vines and Roses," repeated Valerie with evident concern. Vines and Roses is the town's boarding home, run by Erma Puckett. Problem is, Erma's pushing ninety and in no way equipped to handle a crazy woman. "I'll help Andrew and Hannah close up, Kay," said Valerie. "Why don't you go check on Erma?"

I did want to check on Erma; my momma had been friends with Erma since she'd shown up in town the year before I was born with a suitcase full of money and an endless supply of spunk. It was unheard of, back then, for a single woman to buy a home, particularly one as fine as old Dr. Leary's, and the fact she was black, combined with the fact she'd paid with cash, made it all the more a mystery. Rumors aside, however, she'd done wonders for our little town. She was like family to me; I couldn't let her deal with a crazy woman by herself.

"I thank you, Valerie," I said, untying my apron. "I believe I'll do just that."

Chapter 4: Erma Puckett

I was sitting in my rocker on the porch, wrapped up in my afghan and enjoying the cold evening air, when Kay Langley came up the walk. I was always glad to see Kay.

I'd been right close to her momma; she'd been one of the first to welcome me to town all those years ago, and given I own the boarding home and she owned the diner, we were often thrown in together trying to meet the needs of the town. Peggy Mitchell had been one fine woman, always slipping food to those in need when no one was looking. Kay was the apple that hadn't fallen far from the tree.

"Thought maybe you could use this," Kay said, coming up the steps and handing me a steaming cup of hot cocoa. She took a seat in the rocker next to mine. "Heard it's been busy over here tonight."

I accepted the mug with gratitude and a chuckle. "It's not too bad," I replied. "Geraldine got back from visiting family in Memphis today, but you know Geraldine. She don't let me wait on her." Geraldine Pritchett had moved into my boarding home the previous year, leaving her moonshining in-laws behind and reuniting with her estranged daughters. It's a good situation, with Geraldine. We get on well; I was glad to have her back.

"What about Joseph?"

Now, I won't lie, that question made me uncomfortable. Joseph Ammons is my gentleman friend. We'd found each other again after more than half a century apart, and that fact is so special to me I almost hate sharing it. But in a town as little as Cedar Hollow, there isn't much chance of keeping a secret. "He's here," I answered, and try as I might, I couldn't keep the smile out of my voice. "Sleeping. In his room," I said, because Kay kept grinning at me. "Where he stays."

"Well," said Kay, all sassy-like, "I don't mean to tell you your business, Erma, but if that's where he stays, I think that's a major mistake on your part."

I nearly choked on my cocoa. "Kay Langley, you never sassed like that when you were younger."

"No ma'am, I didn't," she said, "but you realize I'm pushin' seventy now, don't you? I figure if I'm goin' to sass, now's the time."

I couldn't argue with that, nor could I argue with Kay's opinion regarding where Joseph stayed. But some things will remain private, I don't care how small this town is. My little white lie—if there is one, and I'm not saying there is—is between me and my maker, and I'm willing to bet he'll understand. And if he doesn't, what's that saying? It's easier to ask forgiveness than permission. I was banking on that one.

"Heard you had a new boarder," Kay was saying, and I turned my attention back to her.

"Mmm-hmm. Came in this evening."

There was Kay, looking at me again. "What?" I asked.

"You must know it's all over town. Layin' on the road, laughin' like a hyena, can't stand up ..." Kay reached out to touch my arm. "Erma, you don't have to open your doors to everyone, you know."

I was touched by Kay's concern, but I didn't need it. "She's all right," I told her. "By the time she got here I reckon all that laughing had worn her out. I gave her a room looking out over Crutcher Mountain, built her a little fire in the fireplace. She seemed real pleased with it. She was freezing cold, poor thing. I don't reckon she's used to our cool night air, being from Florida. She thanked me kindly, then shut the door. I haven't seen or heard from her since."

"Is she really crazy? I mean, can you tell?"

I had to laugh at Kay's question. "I don't reckon she's any crazier than the rest of us are at one time or another," I said. "We don't know what she's dealing with; it's not up to us to judge. But I have a question for you," I said, setting my empty cup on the porch rail. "Would you mind asking the church ladies if any of them have a used jacket this woman can have? Mine are all going to be too small, but she's got to have something if she's going to be here any amount of time."

"I'll ask around," Kay said, "but do you think she's goin' to be here that long? I figured she was just passin' by when her car broke down."

"I believe she was," I told Kay, "but I have a feeling she's going to be here longer than she expects. A few days, at least, until Clifford and Maxwell figure out what's wrong with her car. She's going to need that jacket. And maybe a few other things, too."

Kay looked over at me sideways. "I'll find a jacket, but are you sure you're okay with this, Erma? Do you want me to stay with you until she's gone? We don't know a thing about this woman. For all we know, she could be a criminal of some sort."

I appreciated Kay's offer, but I wasn't the least bit worried about our visitor. "She's not a criminal," I said. "She's just somebody having a rough day. We've all had them. Now, I've got to get inside. My bones are freezing in place." Kay stood to help me up, and I gave her a little hug. "You're a good girl, Kay," I said, thinking of her momma.

Kay grinned, gathering up our mugs to take back to the diner. "So are you, Miss Erma."

Sassy little thing.

Chapter 5: Emily Holt

If anyone had told me a month ago—a *week* ago—I'd experience the events of the past few hours I wouldn't have believed them. I'd have thought they were crazy. Of course, that was before I went crazy myself.

Strangely, I didn't feel the least bit embarrassed by my behavior. No, I felt scattered, as if I couldn't keep the pieces of myself together enough to form a coherent thought. There wasn't enough of me present to care how I came across to others. In fact, I barely registered anyone around me. All I felt were vague impressions. The sheriff impressed me as big and anxious. The people in the general store were nothing more than shadows. The little old woman who met me at the door of the boarding home impressed me as quiet. No, quiet isn't exactly right. She impressed me as *still*. I didn't know how to describe what I felt then, and I still don't, today. But in a world in which everything was swirling around me, she was still.

The room I was given impressed me as warm, and for that, I was grateful. I was shivering so hard my teeth clacked together; my fingers, stumbling across the buttons of my blouse, felt frozen solid. I had no idea what time it was; I only knew it was dark outside my window. Lights twinkled on top of a mountain looming in the distance and closer, somewhere below me, I heard the soft voices of women talking and the quiet creak of a chair.

Something about those sounds transported me back in time, to another evening when impressions took the place of coherent thoughts and words. I couldn't have been more than two or three years old, but I distinctly remembered the same feeling of warmth. I also remembered the faint scent of wood smoke and the sound of women's voices. One, I knew, was my mother's, the other my grandmother's. I remembered feeling safe, cradled against my grandmother's chest. She smelled of lavender. My grandmother had always smelled of lavender. I remembered gentle hands, the feel of a soft quilt, and then a kiss, before the memory faded away, leaving in its wake a feeling of profound loneliness.

Behind me, the fire popped and hissed before quieting to a steady crackle, pulling me back to the present. The owner had turned on a bedside lamp when she brought me to the room, but I reached to turn it off. There was something soothing about the firelight, the shadows playing in the corners. I didn't want to see; for some reason, I equated seeing with thinking, and I didn't want to think.

Instead, I finished removing my clothes. I had nothing with me; my suitcase remained in the trunk of the car—I don't know why I hadn't thought to retrieve it— and although the sheriff had been kind enough to offer to buy whatever I might need for the night, I hadn't been able to pull myself together enough to take him up on his offer.

No matter; I didn't need anything. Shivering, I reached for the quilt folded at the foot of the bed and maneuvered an old wingback chair to a spot between the fireplace and the window. I needed the heat of the fire, but there was something mesmerizing about that mountain, with its sparkling lights at the crest. I wrapped myself in the softness of the quilt and watched the lights shimmer in the distance.

The quilt smelled of lavender.

Chapter 6: Noah Holt

My cell buzzed just as Dr. Cortez dismissed us from class. It was not only my last class of the day, but my last class of the semester. Final exams at the University of Florida would begin the following week, and then I was free for the summer. Well, as free as a man *can* be when he's working a part-time job and living with his mother.

"Good timing," I said to my brother Zach. "Did you break your thumbs? I didn't realize you knew how to actually call someone on one of these things." Zachery was famous for avoiding phone calls. Call him, and he'd refuse to answer the phone but respond immediately with a text.

"I did text you," he said, ignoring my little joke. "Twice, but you didn't answer."

"I was in class," I told him. "Lab, remember? No phones allowed. Crusty Cortez don't play."

"Don't play, huh? Nice vocabulary. Is that how they teach you to speak down there in the swamp?"

Zach and I had an ongoing rivalry, not only because we were brothers, but also because when I applied to colleges two years after Zach, I had remained loyal to my home state, whereas Zach had committed treason.

"I see Benedict Arnold has been working on developing his sense of humor," I replied. "Just keep your hound dog away from our 'gators, 'cause you know how that always turns out."

"We'll have a month to fight about it," said Zach, "which is why I'm calling. When are you done?"

I was surprised by both his serious tone, and the fact he let my dig go without comment. "Exams officially end May third, but I'll be done by next Wednesday. You?"

"Next Friday. You going home as soon as you're done?"

"That's the plan. I should be home by lunchtime. Why do you ask?"

"Just wondering. Hey, have you talked to Mom lately?"

I thought back, trying to remember the last time I'd spoken with my mother. Sometime within the last week, no doubt, but I couldn't remember a specific day, which is what I told Zach.

"Are you sure? Because I haven't been able to reach her for days." He sounded worried.

"No, I'm not sure, but I don't think we've ever gone a week without either calling or texting. Hold on and I'll check my phone." I quickly scrolled through old texts and phone calls, surprised to see it had been so long since I'd had any contact at all with my mother.

"I was wrong," I told him, situating the phone back at my ear. "It's been a couple of weeks. She texted me to ask if I was coming home for the weekend, but I had already made plans. I remember thinking at the time she probably wanted us all together because of Dad, you know. The anniversary. But I couldn't see sitting around like that, just ... what? Thinking about it all? I don't want to think about it all. So I told her I couldn't make it. When's the last time you spoke with her?"

"About the same," he said, "and for the same reason. I told her I didn't want to remember Dad by sitting around crying all weekend. She said that wasn't what it was about; she just thought we needed to honor him. I told her I did honor him, every day, in my own way. But maybe we should have gone, Noah. Maybe she needed us to be there."

"So neither of us went, and neither of us have spoken with her in a couple of weeks," I said, a cloud of guilt settling over me. *And neither of us is in the running for Son of the*

Year, I added to myself. "But I haven't tried to call," I admitted, feeling even worse. "Have you?" I dodged my way out of the crowd of students and moved to sit on a bench under the trees.

"Yeah," he answered, and the worry was back in his voice. "A couple of times. I kept thinking about her calling like that, asking if I was coming home. She'd never done that before. It bothered me a little, especially because I could tell she was disappointed; you know how she sounds. I should have gone, but sometimes it's hard to be there at all with Dad gone, and to be there for that reason was just too much ..." His voice trailed off. Our father's death was still a painful topic for both of us. It had been so unexpected, and his absence left a terrible void. A year later I still found it difficult to talk about, and I knew Zach did, too.

"Anyway," Zach spoke again. "I called her a few days later. That Thursday." *The anniversary*, he didn't add; he didn't have to. "But she didn't answer. She didn't return my call, either. I kind of thought she might be mad at me for not coming home. So I called her again the next weekend, and she still didn't answer. And just now, I tried again. Even if I'd hurt her feelings she wouldn't ignore my messages. Mom's not like that."

He was right. Our mother isn't like that. She might get her feelings hurt every now and then when we're not as thoughtful as we should be, but she wouldn't hold a grudge and she'd never ignore a phone call from one of us. "Maybe she lost her phone," I said. "You know she's always losing things. Or maybe she washed it again. Remember when she did that?"

"But wouldn't you think she'd find a way to let us know?"

"She would if she thought about it," I said, "but you know how forgetful she is. Half the time she doesn't even carry her phone with her, and she never thinks to check messages."

"But for two weeks? Come on, Noah."

He had a point, and I could see no matter what scenario I presented, he was still going to worry. Zach had always been more observant than I, maybe because he's the older brother. Responsibility comes naturally to my brother, whereas I sometimes have to be reminded to come out of my own little world and take a look around. I'm a lot like my mother in that way, I think. We both tend to spend a lot of time caught up in our own thoughts, sometimes forgetting to take into consideration the circumstances around us. She wasn't the only one who forgot to check messages or was forever losing things.

Zach, on the other hand, was more like our father. Both had a tendency to worry about things that I—to be perfectly honest—thought ridiculous. Still, Zach's concern was contagious. The more I thought about it, the more two weeks with no contact with my mother seemed odd, especially since it wasn't just me, it was both of us. "Tell you what," I said. "I'd planned on staying here for the weekend, since next Wednesday I'd be heading home, anyway. Some of us were going to get together and hang out. But I'll go home for the night. I can always drive back tomorrow for the parties and stuff."

"You sure you don't mind?" I could hear the relief in his voice. "I'd just feel better if one of us could check on her. I'd go myself, but it's nearly an eight-hour drive from Knoxville. You can get to her quicker than I can. I have to admit, I'm worried about her. It's not like her to not call me back."

"I don't mind, and now you've got me worried, too. I was just on my way back to the dorm. I'll throw a few things in a duffle bag and head out right away. It won't take me but an hour, hour-and-a-half, tops, to get home. I'll call you when I get there to let you know everything's all right."

"I appreciate it, man. I'm sure she's fine, but I just need to hear it. After what happened with Dad, she's all we've got, you know?"

I did know, but hearing him say it caused an involuntary shiver. My concern for my mother jumped from nagging to critical in the space of a second. "Screw packing," I said. "I've got my keys. I'll leave right now. Call you when I get there."

I hung up, then dialed my mother. The call went straight to voicemail. I pocketed the phone and set off for student parking at a jog. Overhead, dark clouds were building for an afternoon thunderstorm, the slight breeze of the morning whipping along the ground, a miniature dust devil pelting my face with sand. I was sure my mother was fine. I just needed to see it for myself.

Chapter 7: Emily Holt

I dreamt of Gregory. He was young and wiry and smelled of cigarette smoke. His hair was light brown, gathered into a ponytail at the nape of his neck and hanging in a straight line between his shoulder blades and down the length of his back, ending just under the back pockets of his jeans. I had been jealous of that hair, even though I witnessed how much trouble it caused him. It was forever getting closed in doors, sat on by strangers, or tangled in stage equipment.

Once, during a fifteen-minute break between sets, Greg took so long in the restroom I worried he'd passed out. He'd been drinking; women were always plying him with free liquor. I had just psyched myself up for a trip into the men's room when he finally emerged, hair streaming water all the way down the backs of his legs. Turned out he hadn't been quick enough when sitting and his ponytail had gone for a dip in the toilet. Thankfully, he quickly explained it wasn't toilet water spreading across the seat of his pants. He'd gathered his ponytail under the faucet and washed it. I can only imagine what the bikers thought about that.

Greg was not a big man, barely five foot nine when he stretched, maybe one-fifty at his heaviest, at the time of his death. I outweighed him during both of my pregnancies, which he found hysterical, conveniently forgetting I was carrying the weight of two, even if one of the two only accounted for seven or so pounds of the extra weight. Pregnant or not, I always felt clumsy around Greg, particularly in those early days.

He was fine-boned and nimble whereas I was thick-jointed and clumsy. His hair was soft and fine; he had never been able to grow much of a beard, much to his chagrin. My own hair was coarse and wiry, damned near untamable, and don't even get me started on the hair removal products I'd invested in over the years. We were physical opposites in nearly every way. I always thought our hands emphasized our differences perfectly: His were beautiful, the hands of a musician, long-fingered and delicate. Mine were short and stubby, the nails chewed down to the quick.

I used to watch his hands, even when he wasn't playing an instrument. Maybe *especially* when he wasn't playing an instrument. In the beginning, everything he did with his hands seemed erotic to me whether it was touching me, brushing his teeth, or planting a garden. They were just as beautiful covered with dirt as they were resting lightly across a keyboard.

His hands never changed, not even when everything else about him did.

In the dream he was beckoning, his graceful fingers summoning me. I tried to get closer to him, but it was as if I were walking through water. The colors became muted and filtered, my movements slow and cumbersome. I kept my gaze locked on his hands, the only part of him I could still see clearly, that, and his hair, which floated around his head as if it were alive, as if he were the male version of an underwater Medusa.

Even in my dream state, I knew that was wrong. Unbeknownst to me, Greg had had all of his hair cut off the night before our wedding. I could still remember the anticipation in the air as I'd walked down the aisle. I'd assumed, of course, people were excited to see us married. But that wasn't it. No, they were waiting for my reaction when I caught my first glimpse of Greg.

I'm sure I disappointed them at first, although I more than made up for it later. At first, I didn't recognize him. I was slightly puzzled the wedding had begun with my groom-to-be nowhere in sight, but I kept walking forward, arm in arm with my father, who knew no more about the situation than I did. Then a man I hadn't recognized turned and smiled, and I screamed. The crowd went wild; it was the re-action they'd been waiting for.

Maybe if I'd been sitting in a pew, witnessing someone else's reactions, someone else's life, I would have thought it funny, too. As it was, I was about to marry a man I didn't even know. I mean, I *had* known him, but who was *this*? It wasn't just his hair; that's what no one ever seemed to un-derstand. It was that by getting rid of his hair he'd changed who he was. I knew it as soon as I saw him. The life I'd envi-sioned for us would never happen, because the man I was marrying was not the man I'd fallen in love with. I had no inkling how I knew that or how it would manifest, but I knew it would. And it did.

I was, I had believed, marrying not just a musician, but a rocker, a man who spent most of his waking hours coaxing music out of patched together equipment in smoky bars filled with drunken patrons. The man I was marrying had dodged beer bottles and bar fights, never missing a beat. A time or two he'd even had underwear thrown at him, once a lacy red thong, once a stained pair of tighty-whities. Another time or two, a woman had thrown *herself* at him. I loved eve-ry single minute of it, had since the first time I'd seen him up on that stage. The smoke, the booze, the excitement, the mu-sic; the whole scene, the whole lifestyle, was intoxicating. I was marrying a *rocker*.

The man smiling at me looked like a banker, and all I could see when I looked at him was a future version of me: perfectly coiffed, dressed in conservative khakis, a pale blue button-down blouse, and sensible loafers, discussing casse-role recipes with a group of similarly dressed women over cups of designer coffee. Not that there was anything wrong with that; it just wasn't what I wanted to be. I wanted to be the wife of a rocker. I think had my father not had such a tight grasp on my arm, I'd have turned and run. I've often wished I had, but then I think of Zachary and Noah and give thanks for my dad's firm grip.

It's interesting to me that even though I hadn't seen Gregory's fabulous hair since before we were married, it kept showing up in my dreams, live and three-dimensional. Freud once tried to pull together a complicated, far-fetched theory, likening the fear a man faced when first gazing upon Medusa with the fear a boy faces when first gazing upon female genitals. Apparently in both cases what it boils down to is that women are so scary and dangerous men are afraid the johnson might fall right off, or if not that, at least be rendered dysfunctional.

While I generally think Freud should have spent more time on the couch as opposed to beside it, I think he may have been on to something with that one, although the dreams were much too late to do me a damned bit of good. I wonder what he would have thought of an underwater man with Medusa hair?

Anyway, there I was again, slogging through dream-water trying to reach Gregory, when as always, just as I drew close enough to touch him, there was a horrible ripping sound and he was sucked backwards into a watery vortex, his beautiful hands and serpent-haired head obscured by a churning, bubbling maelstrom.

I awakened with a gasp, the air caught in my throat as if it were I who was drowning instead of Gregory. But he hadn't drowned, or at least that's what the autopsy findings said. He'd died of a broken neck, whether caused by the impact with the rail or the water was anybody's guess. Well, I don't suppose *anybody's*, but the coroner didn't seem to know. What he did know was there was no water in his lungs, or at least not a clinically significant amount. Regardless, my subconscious seemed to be acting on the belief that handing me near-nightly dreams of simulated drownings was, for whatever reason, a good idea.

When the dreams first began, a week after Gregory's funeral, I woke up sobbing. This went on for months. I was afraid to go to sleep. I felt such horror, such guilt that I couldn't reach Greg before he was sucked into the gurgling whirlpool. But that night at Vines and Roses, huddled in my lavender scented quilt with the hint of an oncoming crick in my neck, I was no longer sobbing, nor was I guilty. I was mad as hell.

You're dead, you bastard, I whispered in the quiet of my room. *If I couldn't save you when you were alive, what makes you think I can save you when you're dead? Leave me the hell alone.*

Then I gathered my quilt around me, threw a log on the dying fire, and took one last look at that twinkling mountain before crawling into bed. I slept soundly through the rest of the night.

Chapter 8: Zachary Holt

I didn't sleep at all that night, never even made it to bed. We didn't know where our mother was. Noah had made good on his word and reached our mother's house by late afternoon the previous day. He said he'd felt better just driving down her street. Everything looked fine. Mrs. Yarbrough was out watering her flowers and the Spindlers' dog was peeing on our mailbox. A typical day on Palmetto Street. Until he noticed the Spindlers' dog wasn't peeing on the mailbox, *per se*, but on a pile of mail underneath it. The hinged door was open, and even from his vantage point, he could see the box was stuffed to capacity, overflowing onto the sidewalk.

Still, the alarm bells weren't quite sounding yet. The yard wasn't in terrible need of a mow, the hedges were all more-or-less trimmed, and the planters were relatively free of weeds. But then he reached the driveway, and that's when things really began to look odd.

The first thing he noticed was the newspapers. There were eight of them gathered in the dip at the end of the drive, soaking in a puddle from the afternoon storm. Over a week's worth of newspapers marinating in the rain. Definitely weird, he thought, but not yet a reason to enter panic mode. He turned in, running over the papers with a mushy *squoosh*, and pulled around the side of the house to the garage. Which, he said, was open.

At first, he hoped the open garage was a good sign. Maybe our mother was home, after all. As he'd stated earlier, she had a tendency to be absentminded. Maybe she'd simply neglected to pick the papers off the drive. It wasn't unheard of for a paper or two to end up in the recycling bin never having been read, too dirty and weathered after a day or two in the driveway to risk unwrapping.

But *eight*? Besides, he'd said, he'd been so hopeful at seeing the open garage door he hadn't initially noticed the car was gone. My father's Camaro was parked on the right side, a spot from which it hadn't been moved in over a year, but my mother's late-model Toyota was missing. Noah had parked, then gone through the open garage and entered the door leading into the kitchen, which was also unlocked. Initially, he said, everything looked fine. But then he began to smell the rotted fruit.

For as long as I could remember, my mother had kept a bowl of fruit on the counter. Apples, pears, bananas, oranges. They got eaten, too, if not straight out of the bowl, in one of the recipes my mom used to make sure we didn't waste anything. Applesauce, banana bread, orange juice, it didn't matter. One way or another, my mother would make sure we ate enough fruit.

Noah said what wasn't completely blackened and oozing was moldy and soft, and fruit flies and ants covered everything. *That* was definitely not normal. Cue panic mode. My mother hated insects of any kind, which often made living in Florida difficult for her. I once asked her how a person who nearly had a stroke at the site of a ladybug had ever ended up living in Florida. "Trust me," she'd said, "it's not a place I'd ever planned to go. It was fiftieth out of the top fifty states I'd be willing to live in." Descriptive, but not exactly an answer to my question.

That was when Noah backed out of the house and called me. I'd just gotten back to the dorm after a run; otherwise, I'd have missed his call. I felt relief at seeing his name, sure he was calling to tell me Mom was fine and I'd been worried for nothing. It wouldn't have been the first time. You know how every family labels its members? Well, I was the neurotic. Junior neurotic, I should clarify. My dad also obsessed, about everything. When he died, my obsessing increased exponentially, as if I'd agreed to pick up his slack and add his anxiety to my own. It made sense, if you thought about it. After all, one of the biggest things I'd worried over was losing one of my parents. We all know how that turned out.

"So what do I do?" Noah had asked "She obviously hasn't been here for days, unless … God, Zach. I don't want to go in and look." The hitch in his voice was evident, and my blood pressure skyrocketed.

"Call the police," I told him. "Don't go back in. You can ask for a check; I think it's called a 'health and wellness' check, or something like that. Tell them everything that's happened. Our conversations, you going home early, the newspapers and open door, everything. I'm coming home; I'll leave right now."

"Thank God," said Noah. "I really don't want to deal with this alone. But Zach, where do we go? What if we can't stay here?"

"One thing at a time," I told him. "First, call the police. Then, call me and tell me what's going on. After that, we'll figure out what to do next. If I leave now"—I calculated the time in my head—"I should be home by two in the morning, three at the latest. Oh, and when you call the police, tell them about Dad, about it being the one-year anniversary of his death." I hated even saying the words aloud. It was easier to pretend he wasn't dead if I never said the words. "Tell them Mom hasn't been herself, and we're worried she might do something crazy."

"Do you really think that?" Noah's voice climbed an octave on the last note.

I hadn't, until I'd said it. "Telling them that will make them take it more seriously," I said.

"But do you really think she'd do something crazy?" He wasn't going to let it go.

"Maybe," I admitted, "but not something dangerous. Mom wouldn't go crazy like an ordinary person would."

Noah actually laughed, a little too loud, but it was a laugh, nonetheless. "She wouldn't, would she? Remember the rain dance?"

Of course I did, and I told him so. When we were younger, my mother had this crazy dance she'd do every time it rained. She'd twirl and spin and do ballet-style leaps down the hallway, and if the rain wasn't accompanied by thunder and lightning, she'd skip her way barefoot through the yard and dance a jig in the puddle at the end of the drive. When Noah and I were little, we thought she was hysterical. "Do the dance, Mommy," we'd plead anytime we saw the storm clouds building. We'd do it with her, the three of us splashing until we were sopping wet and covered with silt.

The last time I'd seen her do the rain dance I'd been thirteen and Noah eleven. We'd taken the bus home from school and I saw her even before the bus began to slow. We lived three houses down from the bus stop, and there was my mother, waiting for us. She was waving and doing her dance, twirling like a maniac with her hair slicked back from the rain and a grin plastered across her face.

The bus driver had laughed, calling something out to her. I don't remember what he said, but I remember she laughed in return. As for me, I'd been mortified. I hadn't spoken to my mother for the better part of two days. "What's wrong with you?" Noah had asked. "She was just playing around." But I was unforgiving.

The really stupid thing was, even if any of the kids had noticed, they wouldn't have cared. Noah and I had always had the cool mom, the one everyone else wanted to have. Kids *loved* our mother. Our mother arranged ice cream sundae parties when we had company. She was the only parent who allowed us to stay up all night during sleepovers. She went on all of my field trips, and everyone always wanted to be in my group. "Your mom's so *funny*," they said, "so *cool*," but at the age of thirteen, none of that mattered to me. What mattered was my belief that my mother could have irreparably damaged my reputation, and I hated her for it.

When my father emerged from the office one evening a couple of days later, I told him about the incident. I was still irritated with my mother, even though not a single person from school had said a word about it. Unlike my mother, my father was always reserved in public, standoffish, even. I felt certain he'd understand my embarrassment, and I'd been right.

"Emily," he'd called to my mother when I finished making my complaint. She came to stand next to him in my doorway, and something about the way she stood told me she also knew he'd side with me. "Don't you think it might be a little embarrassing to have your friends see your mother dancing in the front yard?"

My mother didn't answer him; she just looked at him with an expression I didn't recognize. My father scratched at the back of his head the way he always did when he was uncomfortable. "Em," he said. "Just think about it from his point of view."

I laid down my pencil, homework forgotten. *Uh-oh,* I remember thinking. *This could get ugly.* My parents never really fought, not the way some parents do, but I could nearly feel the crackle of my mother's anger. I don't know what I thought she'd do, but if I'd been expecting the parental version of Armageddon, I'd been wrong. All she said was, "His? Or yours?"

My father stood fiddling with the buttons of his shirt, and I remember feeling slightly uncomfortable, as if two conversations were happening: the one I could hear, and the one I couldn't. I didn't know what was going on between the two of them, but I wished I'd never dragged my father into it. They were obviously having some sort of silent fight I couldn't understand, and I was sorry to be the cause of it.

"No," my mother finally said, "we certainly wouldn't want them to be embarrassed by a parent." She stormed off down the hallway, leaving us to stare after her.

"I'm sorry," I said to my dad, unsure what I was sorry for but eager to fix whatever was wrong.

He put a hand on my head. "It's not you," he'd said before retreating back into his office, leaving me confused and unsettled.

I'd heard stories of their younger days, how they'd met in a bar where my father's band was playing. It was hard for me to picture my father in a band; he'd always been so discreet and removed. But my mother, if I looked past the *mother* part, I could see without too much trouble. My father had noticed her immediately, he'd told us one night in a rare sentimental mood. It was hard not to, with her wild curly hair and red cowgirl boots. She'd jumped right up on the stage with the band and danced until the end of the set. My father said she'd received a standing ovation at the end, but she swore the applause was for the band. It was odd, watching them tell that story. They looked at each other, smiling, eyes shining, and I remember being uncomfortable in the way kids often become uncomfortable when witnessing parental displays of affection. I wanted them to go back to normal, where they didn't look at each other and Noah and I were the center of the universe.

I felt sorry, remembering those old family stories. For the first time, I had an idea what people meant when they said the thing you loved the most was also the thing you ended up hating. I didn't think my dad hated my mother, not by a long shot. But it seemed to me that while it may have been her sense of fun that pulled him in, it embarrassed him at the same time. I don't think he understood or appreciated her lighter side. He was uncomfortable being the center of attention—something he and I had in common—but my mother had a way of drawing attention to herself, and to us by proximity, at least when I was younger. I had resented it at times, and I knew my father had as well.

My father's death had to have been difficult for her, but she wasn't one to confide in her sons. She worried too much about us to burden us with whatever she might be going through. Besides, she'd never been the sort of person to discuss their relationship openly. I honestly didn't know how his death was impacting her. In spite of that, knowing my mother as I thought I did, I could see her doing something a little crazy on the anniversary of my father's death. Not bad crazy, just crazy.

"Okay. Health and wellness check." I heard Noah take a deep breath. "Zach?"

"Yeah?"

"Be careful, okay?"

"You too, little brother."

"Love you," he said, something we'd always said to each other until ... when? I didn't know exactly when we'd stopped saying it.

"Love you, too. And Noah? It'll be okay," I said, before disconnecting and grabbing my keys. I hoped I was right.

Chapter 9: Emily Holt

I awakened to the sound of birds singing somewhere outside my window. I couldn't remember the last time I'd been able to hear birds chirping from inside a building; for a while, I just lay there and enjoyed the experience. It was impossible to know how early it was. The room was in shadow, but we were in a valley, after all. For the first time in forever, I felt rested, which led me to believe it might have been later than indicated by the peaceful stillness. It was nice to lie there, watching the shadows from the trees play against the wall.

Before long, however, the smell of eggs and sausage made its way under my door and into my nose. That was something else I couldn't remember experiencing. When was the last time I'd lain awake in bed and smelled breakfast cooking? For that matter, when was the last time I'd eaten sausage and eggs? In my never-ending battle against the bulge, I'd gotten used to eating cardboard-flavored cereal and chalky-textured yogurt. But that smell was absolutely heavenly.

I sat up, reaching for my phone to look at the time only to discover the screen black, the battery dead. The charger, of course, was in my suitcase. I hadn't worried too much about charging it since I hadn't had decent reception for days, but I did need to call the kids and check in. I doubted they'd even realized I was gone, but I knew they both had finals in the upcoming week and I wanted not only to wish them luck, but also to find out when I could expect them home.

Home. I hadn't thought of the word, or the place, in days. Was I even going home? I missed my boys terribly, but that was nothing new. I always looked forward to having them home, but the thought of returning to the house on Palmetto Street made my stomach clench. I obviously hadn't been thinking clearly when I'd left, but one thing I knew for certain: I didn't want to return to that house. As crazed as I might have been—might still be—my subconscious had somehow known to get me out of there.

Where, then? I hadn't a clue, but that had been the purpose of the whole trip. I'd drive until I found a home. *My* home. I had no idea where it would be, but I felt certain I'd know it when I got there. Unfortunately, I hadn't taken timing into account. What now? Return to Jacksonville for the summer and resume my trip in the fall? I couldn't imagine returning, but I also couldn't imagine not being with my boys. I had no idea what to do; hopefully I'd have a better idea by the time my car was fixed.

Thoughts of my car pulled me from bed. I didn't even know where they'd taken it, but I felt sure the nice old lady who'd shown me my room would. I reached for my sweatpants and realized there was no way I could wear them without a wash. My blouse, too. They were caked with mud. Had I really been that out of it? I supposed I had, which made me smile.

Wrapping the quilt back around myself I cracked open the door, hoping to see the old woman. What I saw instead was my suitcase, propped against the wall beside my door. Giving a silent prayer of gratitude, I grabbed the handle, stepping into the hall and searching for a bathroom and the comfort of a long, hot shower.

Half an hour later, showered and dressed, I left my phone charging on the nightstand and made my way down the staircase in search of that tantalizing smell. It really was a beautiful home, I realized, as I paused to take it all in. The previous evening I'd been too tired, stressed, and ... well ...

crazy, to notice much of anything. But this morning, with the sun slanting in the windows, I was able to get a good look at my surroundings.

The entire place seemed to be decorated in antiques, and I was willing to bet they were the original furnishings, oiled smooth and soft over the years. A massive fireplace dominated the main room; I suppose it would be called the sitting room. Overstuffed wingchairs were arranged in conversational groupings, built-in shelves were stuffed with books and board games, colorful rugs were scattered along the gleaming oak floors, and the faintest scent of lilac wafted from a stunning antique crystal bowl placed atop a parlor table in the entryway. Had I studied brochures and planned a trip months in advance, I couldn't have found a place more aesthetically pleasing.

Still, it was the aroma of sausage and eggs that propelled me forward. Following my nose, I ventured through the parlor and took a right into a massive dining room. The sheer size of the room was exaggerated by the smallness of the occupants: Three elderly people huddled at one end of a long, walnut table. They all looked up at my interruption, and I nearly laughed. Had I somehow ended up in a retirement home?

There was the elderly African-American woman who had greeted me the night before, dressed in a simple flowered housedress overlaid with an apron. There was an even older white gentleman, very distinguished, long and thin, his shoulders slightly stooped. And finally, another woman. The word that immediately sprang to mind was *handsome*. Her cheekbones were high and defined and her white hair was gathered in an ornate silver barrette at the back of her neck. Another antique, I was willing to bet, and a beautiful one, at that. But what struck me most was her eyes. They were dark, nearly black, and in spite of her age contained an almost defiant spark. This woman was tough, I knew, without knowing her at all.

I hesitated in the doorway, taking it all in, until the owner called my name.

"Ms. Holt," she said, struggling to rise out of her chair. "Come have some breakfast with us. I didn't want to wake you, but as it turns out, you've arrived just in time."

"I don't want to intrude," I said. Something about this group of elderly people made me shy, a feeling I wasn't at all used to having. Of course, I also wasn't used to showing up at a stranger's house covered with mud while barely clinging to sanity. That may have contributed to my shyness.

"Nonsense," the gentleman said, placing a hand on the owner's shoulder. She fell back into her chair with a grunt of apparent relief as he stood to pull a chair out for me. "We've already got a place for you." He motioned for me to sit.

I complied, charmed by his manners. The woman next to me, the one with the barrette, reached to set a pot of coffee in front of me, an old, stainless steel percolator like my grandmother used to have. I was becoming more and more convinced I was either still asleep, or I'd fallen through a time warp.

"Best cup of coffee you'll ever have," said the old man as he returned to his seat, obviously amused by my surprise. "Goodness, where are my manners? Joseph Ammons," he said, standing again and extending a warm hand across the table. "Call me Joseph. And the lovely lady to your left is Mrs. Geraldine Pritchett."

"Just Geraldine," she said quietly. "Everyone just always calls me Geraldine. I have daughters about your age," she said. "They ran away, too. 'Course they was younger. They just come back a while ago."

I was so taken aback by her announcement I couldn't think of anything to say. Who *were* these people?

She raised her brows, clearly assessing me. "You don't need to look so surprised. You just have that look about you. Comin' into town all by yourself, actin' ... well, I didn't see you and that ain't no business of mine, anyway. Folks around here sometimes like to call you crazy if you act in a way they don't understand, but that ain't somethin' I'd ever do."

She paused, the silence feeling almost like a challenge. I remained quiet; what else could I do? What I wanted to say was, *Lady, you don't even begin to know crazy*, but I held my tongue. I didn't think she meant any harm, and I knew my defensiveness stemmed from my own underlying anger, something that was in no way her fault. Besides, maybe she did know crazy; who was I to say?

"You're divorced." She glanced at my hand.

I'd worn my rings for months after Gregory died; I'm not sure why. Habit, maybe, or more likely, mourning the marriage I'd never had to begin with. The strip of white where they'd been was still noticeable against a calloused tan acquired from years of yard work. "No," I said, too surprised to be tactful. "He's dead."

"Ah," she said. "Well, then. My husband died nearly two years ago now. It ain't easy, is it? Life with 'em ain't always easy, either, but life without 'em has its own difficulties. 'Course, if he hadn't died my girls wouldn't have ever come back."

She stopped speaking as quickly as she'd started, just lapsed into complete silence, stirring her coffee as if she'd never spoken at all. Before I could respond—not that I'd have known *how* to respond—the owner spoke again.

"Geraldine, don't scare our guest away." She turned to look at me, smile lines around her mouth communicating her amusement. "One thing you'll learn when you're surrounded by old folks is that whatever it is we're thinking tends to come right out of our mouths. I reckon we're just too tired to bother keeping it in. Now, you and I were properly introduced last night," she said, shooting a sideways look at Joseph Ammons, "so not all of us have forgotten our manners. But I know you had a lot on your mind, so I'll introduce myself again." She held out a small, dry hand. "Erma Puckett, owner of Vines and Roses." This last was said with obvious pride. I couldn't blame her; it was a lovely place. "Help yourself to some breakfast," she said. "It's getting cold." She set a steaming bowl of gravy in front of me as Mr. Ammons pushed a platter of biscuits my way.

"Oh," she said, as if just remembering something, "Clifford called this morning. Said your fuel pump went out. He'll have to order one from Huntington. He said he'd place the order today, but it won't ship out until Monday. They don't ship on weekends. If everything goes right, he said your car should be ready by Tuesday, Wednesday at the latest."

"Tuesday," I said, thinking. "And today is ..."

"Saturday, last time I checked. Looks like you're going to be with us a few days."

"Is the room available for that long?"

She laughed. "Honey," she said, "the room is available for as long as you want it. Geraldine and Joseph have their rooms permanently, but that still leaves two others, and we're not exactly on the beaten path."

I nodded, my thoughts muddled. I needed to check in with the kids sooner rather than later. I also needed to figure out what I was going to do. "Mrs. Puckett—"

"Erma," she corrected me.

"Erma," I began again. "Is there a phone I can use? I haven't gotten good reception since midway through Georgia. I need to call my kids; they'll be coming home from college soon, and ... " I let the rest trail off. *And ... what?*

"There's one in the kitchen and one on the table in the entryway. Use either one of them anytime."

From somewhere in the house, a clock chimed the hour. I was surprised to realize it was only eight o'clock; I'd assumed it was much later. "Thank you," I said. "I'll give them a couple more hours to sleep before I call. They both like to sleep in on weekends. I suppose I should go check on my car while I wait. Is the garage within walking distance? Is it even open today?"

"Just about everything here is within walking distance," said Erma. "As it happens, Hager's is just across the street. As for being open, where else would Clifford and Maxwell be?"

Yet again I found myself unable to answer, so I reached for another biscuit instead, knowing I'd regret it but unable to stop myself. "That mountain," I said, changing subjects, "the one with the lights on top. Is it close?"

"Oh, you mean Crutcher Mountain," Erma answered. "That's the children's lodge you're seeing. You can walk it; just follow Main Street to Deer Jump and go left. You'll go past the old mine, but don't go in there. It's dangerous.

Haunted, too, some say, if you believe in such things. Anyway, from Deer Jump it's about a mile to Platte Road, which'll take you up the mountain. But you can't just wander around up there on account of the kids. You'd have to check in with the front office first."

"What is it, like some kind of reform school or something?" As beautiful as the mountain had looked from my window, visiting with a group of juvenile delinquents wasn't something I wanted to do.

"No, honey, it's a ... what do they call it, Joseph?"

"Retreat. The kids go for a week at a time."

"Right. A retreat. It's for kids with disabilities. They do all kinds of activities. Go hiking, meet new friends, take some therapy, that kind of thing. It gives their parents a break, too."

What a sweet idea, I thought. "Do they ever come to town?"

"Oh, sure, about every week they bring a new group to Kay's for ice cream. Jessie, she's the owner, you know, she comes with them when she's in town."

It amused me the way people in the town threw out first names as if any- and everyone knew who they were talking about. *We'll pick up whatever you need at Mr. Smith's* the sheriff had said. *Why don't you take her to Erma's*, the man at the store had said. *Clifford called about your car. They come to Kay's for ice cream. Jessie owns the lodge.* I guessed in a town that small it was easy to forget someone might not know everyone.

Of course, I had a few days to kill. The town was so small by the end of that time I'd probably know everyone, too, and the first one I needed to meet was Clifford. I'd help clean up the dishes, I decided, and be on my way.

But first, I wanted some more of that gravy.

Chapter 10: Noah Holt

As it turned out, we were able to stay at the house. It isn't like it is in movies or on TV, where you have to wait twenty-four hours to file a report. I filed one right after the police came, after they'd searched the house and found no sign of my mother. They didn't suspect foul play, or at least didn't give me any indication they did, and they certainly didn't treat our home as a crime scene, but Zach had been right; telling them I was worried for my mother's mental health did seem to make them take things more seriously.

Some of their questions were easy to answer. Yes, she'd taken her purse and cellphone. Yes, she'd packed a suitcase. Yes, I could give them a recent picture and provide a physical description. Others were more difficult, and I found myself cringing at my answers. No, I didn't know how long she'd been gone, although I could guess by the number of papers in the driveway. No, I didn't know when she'd last been seen, or by whom, but I hadn't spoken to her for a couple of weeks—thirteen days, to be exact—and Mrs. Yarbrough down the street hadn't seen her for at least that long. No, I didn't know what she'd been wearing, and looking through her clothing didn't help. Jeans and some sort of t-shirt was my guess, but that was only because that's what she always wore.

"Has she been acting out of character?" one of the officers asked, a question that further stumped me. What *was* my mother's character? I'm ashamed to admit I had to stop and think about that question, and the more I thought about it, the more I was bothered by the answers.

In my earliest memories, my mother was fun and unpredictable. She was the one who would check us out of school unannounced and take us to the beach. "You can learn just as much here," she'd say, "and have a better time doing it." She was free spirited, although I'd never previously thought of it in those terms. She was a baby of the sixties born just a little too late to participate in the movements of that time. My mother was the one—against my father's wishes—who not only allowed us to finger paint the wall in our shared bedroom, but encouraged it. "Why not?" I remember her asking my father. "It's their room. Let them express themselves."

It used to drive my father crazy, but my mother always seemed to win out in the end, mainly, I think, because my father just gave up. I remember once, after a trip to the beach, we left half a dozen starfish drying out on the back porch. We were awakened that night by an incredible racket, knocks and bangs and scrapes. Zach and I, convinced someone was breaking through the back door, hid under our beds until my mother came to find us, laughing at what they'd discovered. A raccoon had managed to break through the screen of the porch and topple the patio table. "It's eating the starfish," my mother said. "I know you wanted to save them, but you have to see this. It's so cute, the way she's sitting there holding the starfish with both paws."

"What did you expect?" my father asked, as he grumbled and muttered his way back to bed. "You've got a seafood buffet going on out there."

But my mother wasn't bothered in the least. "Boys, turn out the light for a better look," she said, and we did, building a pallet of pillows and blankets on the floor just inside the sliding door for a close up view of the carnage. We stayed there the rest of the night, an impromptu campout with our mother.

By the time I entered high school our campouts and surprise trips to the beach were over. I don't remember when it happened. Honestly, I don't even remember noticing that it *had* happened. If I thought about family dynamics at all during those years it was mainly to chafe at rules I found unfair or to resent intrusions I felt unnecessary. Zach and I were close enough in age to run with the same crowd and close enough in personality to enjoy each other's company. Our teen years were filled with friends, sports, cars, and the occasional girlfriend. Had anyone asked, I'd have said I was a happy kid from a close family who had an awesome life. It was only normal for my parents to fade into the background at that time.

Wasn't it?

When my father wasn't traveling for his job, he nearly always worked from home. On those days, he stayed holed up in his office, the *studio*, as he called it. We knew not to bother him; we'd always been taught to keep our distance when Dad was working. Entire days would pass with only a glimpse or two of him entering or exiting the studio, his hair standing on end, clothes rumpled and dirty. That was the way my father had always looked when he was in the middle of a project. The Creative Genius, we called him, and he definitely fit the part.

Other times, when he was between projects, he made a point of spending time with us. He'd help us work on a car or practice our golf swing. He'd take us to soccer practice and stay to watch. He loved to talk music with us; he could go on for hours. If he hadn't spent as much time with us as we might have liked, it was only because he worked so hard to support us and give us all the things we needed—and a heck of a lot of the things we wanted.

I don't know what my mother spent her time doing during those years, and I realize that's a terrible thing to say. I honestly never thought about how she spent her days and evenings while we were out on the town with friends. I assumed she did house-type stuff like cleaning and grocery shopping, all the things no one notices are being done until they aren't. If she wasn't as fun-loving and spontaneous as she'd once been, well, we were all getting older, right? We weren't little kids to entertain with nursery rhymes and inger paints. It never occurred to me to wonder if my mother missed having someone to play with.

She ran the house and took care of all of us, even after Zach and I both left for college. She sent spending money and care packages; she cooked for us and helped with our laundry when we came home. She spoiled us; there's no doubt about that. As far as I could tell, nothing had changed for her since my father's death. She was always there for us when we went looking for her; slightly ditzy, scatterbrained as she'd always been, puttering around weeding the flower-beds or trying out a new recipe. That was really all I'd no-ticed, a fact that made me feel worse by the minute.

In the end, I bypassed the officer's question, stammering something along the lines of, "I don't really know. I mean, it was out of character for her to ask us to come home. She's never done that before. But other than that, I couldn't say."

The officer patted me on the shoulder, told me to call if I discovered anything helpful, and promised to be in touch.

By the time Zach got there the officers had long gone. I'd found some frozen pizza in the freezer and cooked it, saving half for my brother. I'd thrown out the rotten fruit along with several items from the refrigerator, some recognizable, some not. I'd taken out the garbage, collected the mail (leaving peed-on envelopes to dry in the garage), and thrown away the newspapers. I'd even made my mother's bed, an action that for some reason made me slightly uncomfortable but which I knew would amuse her had she known. I had an overwhelming urge to make the house as it always had been, as if my mother were there.

When I could think of nothing else to do, I'd spent the remaining wait alternating between pacing and flipping mindlessly through channels, searching for anything to take my mind off the situation at hand. My texts to her remained unanswered; my calls continued to go straight to voicemail. By the time Zach arrived at close to three in the morning I was nearly out of my mind with worry.

He was clearly exhausted, but in spite of the late hour, suggested we go through her desk, looking for any clue as to where she might have gone. We poured through old phone bills and credit card statements, examined calendars and email, and even checked search engines in hopes she might have planned a vacation about which she simply forgot to inform us. At first we found nothing.

But then we did, although it took a minute or two for us to figure out what, exactly, we'd found. A large manila envelope, one I'd even pushed out of my way a few times as I'd examined the contents of the drawer. It was thick and heavy, with my father's name scrawled across it in his handwriting, the handwriting the reason I hadn't paid closer attention. After all, we were looking for information regarding my mother, and we'd by that time gotten somewhat used to seeing my father's belongings boxed up or otherwise packaged away.

Zach was the one who pulled it out, frustrated, I believe, that it kept getting in the way. Exhausted and cranky—understandably so—he didn't so much remove it from the drawer as fling it. "God," he said, "what *is* this, anyway?" The smack of it against the wall is what captured my attention.

Tired, worried, and convinced we wouldn't find any helpful information in our current search, I walked over and picked up the envelope, sliding to sit along the wall. Opening the clasp and running my finger against the tape, I opened it and pulled out the contents.

"Zach," I said after a moment or two. "You should take a look at this."

Chapter 11: Emily Holt

The flowers were beautiful. I didn't know what kind they were. Bulbous buttercups, I thought, conjuring a memory from somewhere, a flower many considered a nuisance. *A weed is but an unloved flower.* Who had said that? Wilcox, I remembered, Ella Wheeler Wilcox, a turn-of-the-century American poet. Those who considered bulbous buttercups to be a weed had obviously never seen a sight such as the one before me. The plants spread across the meadow in glorious form, shadows from the surrounding mountains only serving to highlight the brilliant gold of the foliage. I stopped in my tracks at the sight, moving off the trail and climbing to sit on a boulder to take in the view. It was breathtaking.

I'd visited the repair shop (*Shoppe*, I reminded myself) and then, with time to kill, followed Erma's directions to Crutcher Mountain. But I wasn't in the mood for company, be it kids or adults, so when I saw a hand-lettered sign for Rugged Creek, I decided to follow it instead.

Rugged Creek, as it turned out, was a meandering, rocky, perfectly lovely creek that made its way downhill between two mountains, one of which I assumed was Crutcher Mountain; I didn't know if the other had a name. Where the creek went from there I also didn't know, but vowed to one day find out. I was inexplicably curious, maybe due to the exquisite setting, or maybe because I'd always been a decorator at heart and in spite of the years, the surroundings tapped into that part of me. Nothing manmade, however, could have competed with the scene in front of me.

I settled further back on the boulder, enjoying the feel of the sun on my shoulders. The morning was chilly, but I found it invigorating. I couldn't remember the last time I'd had so much energy. I had avoided thinking of the future for the better part of a week, but I needed to make some decisions. As much as I'd enjoyed the absolute freedom of the past few days, I couldn't run away forever.

The hardest part, of course, would be talking to my children. If there was one thing Greg and I had agreed on, it was the need to protect our children. Greg had been adamant they not know the darker parts of our marriage, and I had supported him in that belief. But now Greg was gone and our children were no longer children; there were things they had a right to know. They needed to be able to monitor themselves. They needed to be able to monitor their children. I just needed to figure out how to tell them.

I had been right about Gregory's hair. That was the part I kept going back to, had been going back to for nearly the entirety of our marriage. As silly and superstitious as it may have seemed for me to connect the loss of the ponytail with the loss of the man, I'd been right. At least, it had marked the loss of the man I'd known the six months we'd dated, but really, what does anyone know about anyone after only six months?

I was dabbling in interior decorating back then, just starting out and eager to make a name for myself. A friend of a friend recommended me to the owner of a little bar and grill on the south side of Denver. I'd seen the place before; I'd grown up just a few miles farther south, in Black Forest, so I knew the bar was a dump. It needed much more than a decorator could offer, but I was young and eager and optimistic and besides, paint can cover a lot of flaws.

My work was done in the mornings, before the bar opened for business, so it was only by chance I met Gregory. He came in early one morning as the owner and I were debating seat covers. The bar needed new ones, but the owner couldn't afford them. I couldn't think of a way to work torn and stained red vinyl seats into my beautiful southwestern-style plan. "It'll give it an authentic look," the owner said with a lopsided grin.

"Right," I said, "if what you're going for is an authentic dump."

"That's a little harsh."

"Look. I'm good, but I'm not a miracle worker. It doesn't matter what I do to this place, if you don't replace the seat covers it's still going to look like a dump."

Our debate was interrupted by a knock on the bar's back door. "That'll be the singer guy," said the owner before disappearing behind the bar, presumably to invite the singer guy in.

I was on my hands and knees peering under a booth when in walked Greg. "Now, that's a position I like," was the first thing he said to me, and I looked up to see an almost frail looking young man with amazing hair and tattooed arms.

"Go screw yourself," was the first thing I said to him.

"Feisty," he responded. "I like that, too."

We connected immediately; how could we not? We were both young entrepreneurs, both scrambling to make a living with our own sort of art. We were even dressed alike, in so much as we could be: jeans, sleeveless t-shirts, and boots. We were free thinkers, artists, radical liberals in a conservative town, or at least that's how we liked to think of ourselves. We were nonconformists, blind to the irony of the immediate connection either of us experienced when we met someone just like us. We were meant for one another, or so it seemed. And when all was said and done, maybe we had been. Just not in the way I'd originally thought.

I lay back on my boulder and watched the clouds. There was a storm building over the mountains to the east, indigo clouds scuttling across an ever-darkening sky. As reluctant as I was to leave that peaceful place, I had at least a two mile walk ahead of me to get back to the boarding home, possibly even longer. I didn't want to be caught in the storm when it hit, and besides, I felt sure even my lazy boys would be semiconscious by then. I didn't know how to start the conversation with them, but I was determined to try. I took one last look at the meadow, the flowers now weaving and rippling in the increasing wind, and turned to follow the creek back to the road.

More early wildflowers grew along the sides of the trail, blue violets and white clover among the ones I recognized. I decided to pick a handful, trusting Erma would have a little vase, or at least a juice glass, I could borrow. The blues and whites blended so sweetly in my miniature bouquet I was overcome with nostalgia. I remembered warm days in the clear Colorado air, walking with my grandmother. "Look, honey," I heard her say as she stooped over our path. "Dandelions. You know what we can do with these? Have a seat and I'll show you." She patted the ground and we sat as my grandmother taught me to make a necklace from the flowers. By the time we stood to resume our walk I was adorned with chains of yellow, covered nearly from head to foot.

Moved by the memory I wove flowers together as I walked, first creating a necklace, then a wreath for my hair. I was sure I looked ridiculous, but who was to see? For once, I determined, I was going to be who I wanted to be and do what I wanted to do without someone shushing me, warning me not to draw attention. I was so *tired* of living within the boundaries of someone else's need.

Distracted as I was by both the flowers and my memories, I hadn't even made it to the road before the downpour arrived with a vengeance. I could scarcely see; the rain blew in sheets across the trail; the wind whipped my hair across my eyes and tore at the flower chains around my neck. Caught off guard by the sheer velocity of the deluge, I initially thought to jog, to try to reach shelter more quickly. The folly of that plan soon became evident. Jogging hadn't been in my arsenal of activities for longer than I could remember. I'd barely made it to the next curve in the trail before I was completely winded, not to mention soaked to the skin, and the cloudburst showed no sign of letting up.

With no obvious solution at hand, I surrendered to the elements, reveling in the sheer power of it all. I had always loved the rain; the idea of washing the world clean and starting fresh appealed to me. I wasn't afraid; there was no thunder, no lightning, just the pounding, blowing torrent of rain. I turned my face to the sky, gasping as the wind whipped my breath away, laughing as water streamed down my face and fell from my chin.

And then I tripped, of course, because that is the sort of thing I do. I am not the type of person who can throw my arms wide to the world and turn my face to the sky in true *The Sound of Music* fashion and not trip on something. So I tripped, and then I slipped and slid on my belly all the way to the road, my front covered with mud, hands grappling for something to break my fall. Thankfully, I came to rest just before the asphalt, the mud depositing me there before coursing over my behind and continuing down the hill.

The blip of a siren.

Ah, geeze.

The squelching sound of footsteps through puddles.

Well, of course.

The arrival of black oxfords under my nose.

I didn't even bother to look up.

"Still looking for that contact?" The same deep voice as the previous day.

I sighed, rolling over and sitting up in the stream of mud sluicing along the side of the road.

"I'm not crazy, you know," was what popped out of my mouth. I shook my hair out of my face in an attempt to see through the gushing water.

Standing over me, rain dripping from his hat, the officer pursed his lips. "No ma'am," he said. "I'm sure you're not."

I don't know what it was about him that made me want to laugh. Maybe it was because he was so expressionless, so seemingly unflappable. Whatever it was, I had to work to stifle a giggle.

"Ma'am?" he said. "Whatever your fascination is with our asphalt, it's a dangerous hobby to have." He reached down and grasped my elbow, hauling me to my feet. "Let me give you a ride back to Erma's."

"You're a real buzzkill," I muttered, allowing him to lead me to his car.

"Yes, ma'am," he said. "I reckon I am."

And then I did laugh, God help me, all the way to Erma's.

Chapter 12: Zachary Holt

We read the entire envelope before finding five others buried at the back of the bottom drawer of my mother's file cabinet. They covered years, nearly my entire life, and certainly all of Noah's. There's nothing quite like the feeling you experience when you realize the life you've led is only half the story.

I'm not sure what time it was when we turned out the lights and climbed into the bunk beds we'd shared as kids. I do know the sliver of sky showing through the slats of our blinds was just beginning to show more grey than black. Even then, as tired as we were, we were unable to sleep for some time.

"Trip to Sanibel when I was six," said Noah. "You'd have been eight."

"Yep," I said, answering his unspoken question. I knew exactly what he was feeling and also that nothing I could say would change it.

"Remember all the shells we collected? 'Best beach for shells in the whole country,' Mom told us. She was right. We had garbage bags full. Remember?"

"I do."

"Brought 'em home and put 'em all around the patio for decoration."

"Mmm-hmm."

"Dad was working and couldn't go with us. Did he *ever* go on trips with us? I can't remember."

"A couple of times to visit family in Colorado," I said. "But you'd have been really young."

"Yeah, I don't remember him ever going there with us. I just assumed it was because his parents had passed away and it was hard for him to take enough time off work for the trip. He wasn't ever very close to Mom's family, was he?" Noah leaned over the edge of the top bunk to look at me.

"You know, I'm not really sure," I said. "I never heard him say anything bad about any of them. But this whole night has me questioning everything I thought I knew. Like all those private conversations Mom used to have with her parents when we flew out to visit. Remember those? She'd shoo us outside to play so she could have 'grown-up time' with her family. We'd get bored and try to go back in and the door would be locked. We'd have to yell and bang and ring the bell for what seemed like forever before one of them would finally open the door. Then they'd act like they hadn't known it was locked to begin with."

"I'd forgotten about that." Noah fell silent for a moment before asking, "What about that surprise trip we took to the Everglades? Mom picked us up from school with suitcases packed. I was ten. I remember that because Mrs. Collins had given us a project to do over winter break and I was afraid I wouldn't have time to do it. 'You'll be fine,' Mom said. 'Just relax and have fun. I promise we'll get it done before the end of break.' And we did, too. Mom helped me. But maybe we should have suspected something?"

I didn't answer Noah's question because there was no need to. It was a macabre game we were playing, a liar's version of twenty questions. "Dad's conferences," I said. "The one he was required to go to during my graduation."

"Yeah," said Noah, his voice dipping. "That was bad."

That *was* bad. What made it worse was Dad wasn't even the one who told me. Mom was, after Dad had already gone. I had been angry not only because I couldn't imagine anything being worth missing your own son's graduation, but also because Dad hadn't even had the guts to tell me himself.

He'd just packed up and gone while Noah and I were in school, leaving Mom to break the news. "He had to go," she'd said. "You know things have been tense for him at work. They're laying people off, Zach. Your dad can't take that chance. When they tell him he has to attend a conference, he has no choice but to attend."

"But did he explain? Did he tell them I'm graduating high school next week?"

"Of course he did, Zach. He did everything he could, and he feels absolutely horrible about this. But they didn't give him a choice. I'll videotape the ceremony and send it to him. I know that's not the same, but it's the best I can offer. And we'll all take a trip and celebrate when he gets home."

It wasn't the same, and it didn't solve the problem. Dad had missed a lot of our events over the years due to his job, but we'd always understood. When he'd returned from trips, we'd been front and center, almost to such an extent we'd wanted him to back off a bit. But this had been unforgivable. I couldn't imagine a company being so thoughtless as to make a man miss his own kid's graduation, nor could I imagine my father giving up and giving in. Of course, with the discoveries Noah and I had made over the course of the night, I now knew the whole story was a lie. What I didn't know was how to feel about it.

"It must have been awful for him," I said, struggling to integrate our new information into what I'd always believed our reality to be. How much of what I thought I knew was true? Clearly he'd had a job; we'd enjoyed a comfortable middleclass lifestyle. Surely some of those business trips had been real.

Hadn't they?

We'd been raised to believe his work was the cause of his absences. To think he'd deliberately held himself apart to shield us from what he was going through ... It was mind-boggling. "Can you imagine how alone he must have felt?"

"No, I can't," said Noah. "But what about Mom?"

"What about her?"

"I don't know. I mean, that she lied to us, I guess. But not even that. God, Zach, I don't know what I mean. I mean, it's awful, finding out this stuff about Dad, and it makes me feel terrible for him. Guilty, for some reason, you know? Like, we'd get frustrated because we couldn't have company over when he was home. Or we'd get mad when he missed something because he was out of town. But if he couldn't help it ... No, like I said, I can't imagine how he must have felt, but what about her?" I heard him flip over in the bed above me. "I was thinking about all this stuff when the cops were here. They kept asking me if it was out of character for her to disappear. Would you have known the answer, Zach? Because I didn't. Which character? The one from when we were little? Or the one now? They're not the same. *She's* not the same. And do you think she knew, when they got married? Because if she didn't, that would have really sucked."

I hadn't considered that possibility until Noah's question. I thought of my mother, conjuring up images of her. Sadly, Noah was right. The most animated memories were from years and years before. She'd disappeared even before she'd disappeared. That's what she'd done, really. She still took care of us; she did everything for us. As a senior in high school, I remember being embarrassed once when a note of hers fell out of my backpack: *Love you, Zach*, she had written. *Good luck with your presentation. Hope you have a wonderful day!* Signed with hearts and smiley faces.

But the laughing, spontaneous mother, the one who sang off-key and danced embarrassingly and wore dangly cartoon earrings for every single holiday ... I don't know when she disappeared, but she did. Now that Noah had brought it to my attention, I felt partly responsible, even if my responsibility was simply in not noticing.

Realizing that brought the truth home, and it hit me hard. "I don't think she knew, Noah." It was painful to say, as if the admission were a final break from the illusion of childhood. "I really don't think she knew."

"Then she was alone, too," he said. "I'm just saying."

Neither of us spoke then, thinking, I suppose, or maybe trying not to. Eventually, as the light brightened outside our window blinds, we fell asleep.

Chapter 13: Erma Puckett

"Erma," Joseph called to me from the porch, where he'd gone to sit and watch the storm. He does love a good rain, Joseph does, and that was definitely a good one. He'd had to pull the rocking chair all the way back under the window, as far away from the railing as possible to keep from getting soaked by the blowing rain. "Our girl is back," he said. There was a pause before he called to me again in a softer voice, "You might need to come see this."

I rinsed my hands and dried them on my apron. I had thought to make a nice cucumber salad for lunch, something light and crisp. I was ready for spring and there was nothing more spring-like, to my way of thinking, than a cucumber salad sandwich with some juicy cantaloupe on the side, all washed down with a glass of sweet tea. I turned the burner down under the eggs and left the cucumbers on the cutting board before going to see what Joseph was talking about.

I had to laugh when I saw him. He was standing with his back pressed against the wall, shirtfront damp from the rain and droplets hanging from his eyebrows. "Land sakes," I said, catching my breath against the cold wind. "It's going to take more than a cucumber salad to turn this weather into spring."

Joseph smiled. "But isn't it wonderful," he said, "the blessings of nature." That's Joseph, always seeing the blessing in ordinary everyday things. I love that about him, always have. He's a fine man, a retired minister with a gentle soul who found his way back to me after over half a century apart. A man who'd been colorblind at a time when being colorblind could have cost him everything, had I not refused to allow that to happen. My Joseph is a man who stayed loyal to me during all the years circumstances forced us apart.

"It is wonderful," I agreed, linking my arm through his. "I'm flat-out surrounded by blessings."

Joseph stooped to lean his cheek against mine, and I felt his smile against me for a second before he pulled away. "We are indeed surrounded by blessings," he said. "And although one of them hasn't yet been explained to us, she's headed this way, seemingly in need of some assistance."

I looked through sheets of rain to where Joseph pointed and saw Sheriff Moore bending to help our newest boarder from his patrol car. "Lord have mercy," I whispered under my breath, and Joseph chuckled. "He does indeed," he said. "And this one seems to need it."

Emily Holt was plumb covered in mud. Mud, and flowers. Why, she looked almost exactly like one of those little clay gingerbread men Valerie Poindexter helps the children of town make every winter down at the library. Valerie has a whole passel of crafting activities for the holidays, but she is most proud of those ornaments. She lets the kids shape and decorate them with all sorts of sparkles and paint, then she bakes them on low until they're set hard and gives them back to the children the next week to take home to their families.

Now one of those gingerbread men—or women, in this case—was walking toward me, trailing chunks of mud and soggy field flowers across the lawn behind her, looking exactly like one of Valerie's ornaments dripping sparkles and paint. For the life of me, I couldn't think what to say. It was Sheriff Moore who broke the silence.

"Miss Puckett. Mr. Ammons," he said, placing a foot on the lower step of the porch. "How are you this fine afternoon?" As he spoke, his breath blew the rainwater trailing down his face into a fine mist.

"Doing fine, Sheriff, but why don't you all come in from this weather and get warm?" Joseph moved to open the door.

"Oh, I can't go in like this," the gingerbread woman said. "Ms. Puckett, do you have a hose? I can at least rinse the mud off first."

Mrs. Holt's question finally moved me to speak. "The hose is around back," I said, "just outside the laundry room. You rinse yourself off and I'll get you a towel and a robe. Come right up the steps when you're finished and change, and we'll put your clothes straight in the washing machine. Let me run you a bath, too, honey. You must be half frozen."

"Thank you," she said, rubbing at the mud along her front. "It's so cold here; I'm not used to it."

"Well," said the sheriff, and I saw an irritated look cross his face, this man whose feelings were a puzzlement to most of the town, "it's a little early in the season to go playing in mud."

Mrs. Holt squealed and at first I was worried, but then I saw she was laughing. Joseph and I shared a look while the sheriff wiped a hand over his face and stared at the ground. "Mrs. Holt?" I asked, when it finally seemed she'd worn herself out.

"Oh, I'm fine," she said, holding onto her stomach and doubling over with more snuffles and squeals. "He's just so *funny*, is all. Oh, my God, I can't breathe." We waited while she got herself under control. "Okay, I'm going," she said, standing and drawing a deep breath, swiping a muddy arm across her eyes. "Thank you, Sheriff, for the ride. I'm really sorry about your car. I'll pay to have it cleaned."

"Not necessary," he said. "The county will get it. Just ... Mrs. Holt?" He turned to look at her, and I could see his jaw muscle clenching. He wasn't happy, that much was clear. "You really should be careful. These roads are dangerous, with all the curves. What I'm trying to say is, I don't know what exactly it is you're up to, but laying in the road like that, it's just not safe."

Mrs. Holt squealed again, and stuffing a fist into her mouth, lurched around the side of the porch. Standing there in the storm, we could hear her laughter fade away as she rounded the back of the house.

For a few seconds the three of us stood listening, until we were sure she was gone. "Sheriff?" I asked. "You want to come in for a cup of coffee? You're soaked to the bone."

"Thank you, ma'am," he said, "but I think I'm going to head on home to get into some dry clothes. And maybe swap out cars until this one has been detailed." He turned, staring off into the distance. "This town," he said, and shook his head, water flying from the brim of his hat. We waited. "This town is an interesting place." With that, he turned and headed to his car, while Joseph held the door open for me so I could go and see to our guest.

Chapter 14: Emily Holt

I didn't start crying until I saw the old woman bent over a claw-foot tub shaking bath salts into steaming water. I'd followed her directions, hosing myself off before letting myself in the back door to the laundry room and stripping out of my clothes. She'd left a bathrobe for me, just as she'd said she would, and I surrounded myself in the soft folds before starting the washer and gingerly peeking into the kitchen.

It was empty, silent except for the soft ticking of a cooling stove burner recently turned off. Ms. Puckett—Erma, I reminded myself—had obviously been making lunch before she'd been interrupted by yet another of my crazed appearances. I felt guilty for bringing chaos into the lives of these people. That had never been my intention; I just didn't know how to escape it.

I trailed through the living room, relieved to see it also empty, and made my way up the stairs. Erma had mentioned a hot bath, which sounded perfect. I was once again freezing, my teeth chattering hard enough to jar my head. I'd bathe and dress in fresh clothes before finding a phone and calling my boys. I was certain neither of them had planned a visit home over the weekend; they'd likely be splitting their time between studying for exams and partying with friends, but on the off chance they noticed my absence, I didn't want them to worry.

These were the thoughts running through my head when I approached the bathroom and was met with the warm aroma of gardenias, the soft light of a flickering candle, and Erma Puckett, testing the water one last time before turning off the knobs. I don't know what it was about that scene that caused grief to bubble up in my throat, but it did, and it was just as uncontrollable as my hysterical laughter had been only moments before. Wiping my nose against the back of my hand, I wondered briefly how many calories I was burning with my out-of-control mood swings. At least there was that.

"Goodness, you scared me," she said, turning and spotting me in the doorway. "I didn't hear you come up. Now, I've put fresh towels on the rack for you and there's plenty—" She stopped, catching sight of my face. "Oh, honey." She didn't reach for me, for which I was grateful. Instead, she leaned her cane against the wall, put her hands on her hips, and looked me up and down, squinting in the flickering light from the candle.

"I don't know what it is that's working on you so," she said finally, "but one thing I do know. You've got to get your footing. You can't keep going on, stumbling from one day to the next. That's no way to do it. You've got to get your footing."

She patted my arm as she walked by on her way to the door, balancing on her cane to turn back to me. "Take all the time you need," she said, before closing the door behind her with a decisive thump. I was left wondering if she meant I should take my time finding that elusive footing, or if she simply meant in the bath. Both, I hoped.

I slipped off the robe and put a tentative foot in the water before sinking down into the steamy scent of flowers with a sigh and a sense of relief.

You've got to get your footing, she had said, and although I hadn't thought of it in those terms, she was absolutely right. The simplicity of her statement somehow comforted me, as if my current state were simply a slip, a misstep that could still be corrected.

The truth of the matter was that by the time my husband died, I had absolutely hated him. I'd never admitted that to anyone, had never spoken it aloud, and never even recognized it myself, until the night he died. It hadn't always been that way, of course, but it had certainly been that way for the last few years of our marriage. In the early years, I'd accepted his quirks as just another part of his artistic temperament. Artists are always a little bit crazy, aren't they? It's a part of their genius, or so I'd always heard. Poe, Hemmingway, Woolf, Beethoven, Tolstoy, Plath, and on and on, not to mention a whole slew of speculated cases among modern actors, actresses, musicians, and writers.

If one really thinks about it, how can a person not be a little crazy, baring his soul to the world through his art day after day, year after year, living on a tightrope between success and failure? At the beginning of our marriage a bad day for me meant the car had made a weird knocking noise, I'd gotten a run in my stockings, or a client had been less than pleased with the color palette I'd presented. For Greg I quickly learned, a bad day meant a critic had ripped apart his music, ridiculed him as a hack, or even worse, described him as a poor substitute for some other musician, either dead or alive. My bad days were external; Greg's were internal. Mine annoyed me; his destroyed him.

But even so.

The moods were difficult. I'd burst into the house at the end of a wonderful day and be met by Gregory, sitting alone in the dark and swigging a beer. No, "How was your day?" No, "Honey, glad you're home." In the wake of his despair I couldn't very well say, "My day was fantastic, honey! The Smith's love their new living room and even referred me to their accountant."

From the very beginning, our marriage revolved around Greg's moods, for *moods* is what I thought it was back then. *Greg's always been a little moody,* his own mother said one day when she stopped by and Greg refused to get out of bed to visit. So on those days, Greg's bad days, I began keeping my happiness to myself, shucking it like an extra sweater before entering my own home. What sort of life is that?

But that's not all. Greg also had good days, and his good days were *extremely* good. So good, in fact, he wouldn't sleep for weeks. He'd pace the living room with wild eyes and even wilder hair, scribbling lyrics onto the little notepad he always carried. He'd stay at the studio until all hours of the morning, coming home only an hour or two before I had to awaken, waking me anyway. "Babe," he'd exclaim, "this one is the *one*. This one is going to propel us to the top of the charts."

I'd do my best to wake up and share his enthusiasm, content in the way only a woman in love can be as I went about my duties the next day exhausted but glad, thrilled, even, that Greg was finally making it in the indie musicians' world he so loved. Then I'd inevitably come home one afternoon, maybe a week later, maybe six months, eager to see what news Greg had to share, and find a dark house, Greg alone in the living room again, drinking a beer. "It's pointless, Em," he'd say. "I should just end it all now and get out of everybody's way."

How to describe that feeling? I can't. It's the most hopeless, the most frustrating, *alienating* feeling. There simply aren't words.

By the time I was pregnant with Zach I knew there was a problem, but I still hoped, young optimist that I was, that Greg would find his way, that he'd get that lucky break and the tough times would be behind us. I was still eager to blame it on something external; it was much too frightening to think the problem resided within Greg as opposed to without. Somewhere inside, though, I knew. This was more than moods, more than an artistic temperament. This was something big, something beyond Greg's, or my, ability to control.

I ignored the nagging suspicions those first few years, as did Greg. Back in those days, I was still very much in love with Greg, was even a little in awe of his talents and sensitivities. I was proud to speak of "my husband, the musician." I loved inviting friends and clients to clubs to listen to his band. Make no mistake, he was talented, extremely so. The downfall of Greg's band wasn't due to a lack of talent on any of their parts; it was due to Greg's inability to manage himself.

Bandmates, club owners, bar patrons....It was all the same. No matter how wonderfully things started out, eventually Greg would torpedo any chance of success and then wonder why he couldn't get ahead. Sometimes he had a legitimate gripe, like the time his bass player—the fourth one in less than two years—rode off into the sunset with Greg's equipment. Or the time the club owner was three months behind in paying the band.

But more often, the conflict resided solely in Greg's own head. Nearly anything could set Greg onto the path of self-destruction. An imagined slight, the lack of a smile, a perceived coolness in tone. It never occurred to Greg that maybe the other party was distracted. Maybe the previously friendly bartender was falling behind with his bills; maybe the formerly chatty server was worried about a sick baby at home. Maybe friends weren't always going to be available because they had *lives*. Girlfriends, wives, babies, jobs, just ... *things*.

No, in Greg's mind, it was always about Greg.

Did you see how she avoided me?

Does he seem distant to you?

Did you notice he didn't even shake my hand?

What began as nothing quickly ballooned into something in the wake of Greg's paranoid inability to let it go. Friends and loved ones did their best to be understanding—*Oh, you know Greg, he's a worrywart*—but there comes a time when even the most understanding person grows weary of being falsely accused and forced into a position of defensiveness.

Greg was like a bouncy ball, the kind kids buy from oversized gumball machines for a quarter. Once he got going, he was all over the place with his emotions. I felt terrible for him, we all did, and we all did our best to comfort and reassure him. But in the end people simply couldn't keep up with him; they never knew which Greg to expect. The sad irony of Greg's life: He reacted in such a way to his delusions that they eventually became real.

Do you hate me, Emily?

Of course not. I love you.

I make life so hard for you. You have to hate me.

No, Greg. I'll always love you, no matter what.

Are you seeing someone else? Emily, you're having an affair, aren't you?

How can you even ask that? I would never do that, Greg.

Goddamn it, why can't you just admit it? I know you are. You avoid me. You never come to bed on time. You're nothing but a slut.

What's gotten into you? I've never cheated on you. I never will.

Fuck you, Emily! You're a liar!

You know what, Greg? You're right. Now I do. Now I hate you.

The real kicker is I ended up hating myself even more. *For better or worse,* I'd promised. *In sickness and in health.* I hadn't known when I'd made the promises the *worse* and *sickness* parts would come to dominate our marriage. What kind of wife was I? What kind of person was I, to break my promises to Greg over circumstances he couldn't control?

I railed against Greg and blamed him for all our problems, but I knew, sitting in Erma Puckett's claw-footed tub surrounded by steam and the scent of gardenias, I was the truly despicable one.

Chapter 15: Emily Holt

I stayed in the tub until the water chilled and my toes shriveled. It was the need to call Zach and Noah that finally propelled me forward. As it turned out, I wasn't able to reach either of them. Dressed in a fresh pair of jeans and a sweater, my wet hair dripping down my back, I located the phone in the entryway and left nearly identical messages on both their phones. "Hey, babe, I took a little road trip. I'm in West Virginia at a bed-and-breakfast sort of place. Just wanted to wish you luck with finals. Give me a call when you get a chance to let me know what your plans are. Call me at this number, though; the cell reception here is terrible. Love you."

I hung up the phone reluctantly. I'd really hoped to be able to speak with my boys. They had their own lives now, and I was proud of them for that. But that didn't stop me from missing them.

As I stood in the entryway thinking of these things, I heard voices from the front porch. I was hesitant to face anyone; I felt bad for interrupting their morning, and was more than a little embarrassed for having done so in such spectacular fashion for two days running. But I did want to apologize and thank Erma for her kindness, so I took a deep breath and gathered my courage.

Glancing through the front door, I saw the rain had stopped. Brilliant blue was peeking through the clouds and

everything had that fresh-washed feeling it gets after a tor-
rential downpour. The new leaves were a lustrous shade of
green, the rhododendrons lining the walk a cacophony of
colors: pink, purple, red, petals shimmering with drops in
the iridescent light. Puddles formed along the walk, and a
distant part of me wanted to splash in them, but I'd filed that
part of myself away a long time ago, and the mishap of my
morning only served to reinforce that decision.

Greg had been right; there were times I'd embarrassed
the children, especially Zach. Ironic, that it was their dad's
behavior we strove so hard to hide, but mine that always
ended up embarrassing them. Had it not been so outrageous,
it would have been funny. I suppose it's a testament to our
abilities of deception, their dad's and mine, that they were
never embarrassed by *him*.

If nothing else, Greg and I were masters at publicly
playacting the family we wanted to be. We presented as a
typical suburban family, a bit private, maybe, but nice.
Friendly. Helpful. The kind of neighbors who'd collect your
mail for you while you were on vacation. The kind who'd buy
overpriced wrapping paper and stale popcorn to help support your kid's fundraiser.

Had it been up to me, I may have confided. I may have
welcomed people into our lives—our real lives—in a more authentic way. I never thought people would judge us the way
Greg thought they would. "No family is perfect," I'd tell him.
"Every family has issues they're struggling with, in one way
or another."

"Look at what happened in Colorado," he would counter.
"Look at what happened with my band. Everyone left. Every
damn one."

He was right; they had, but as we grew older and more
settled, as we picked up the mantle of adult respectability
and left our more bohemian past behind, I was convinced
their leaving was less about Greg than it was about their own
lives. They weren't living a lifestyle conducive to standing
still. Neither had we, until we'd had no other choice. They
didn't leave Greg so much as they simply continued moving
after we stopped.

I wanted friends. I wanted a social connection that consisted of more than waving at neighbors from across the street, but maintaining appearances was crucially important to Greg, and our appearance wouldn't have held up to scrutiny. The memories caused a pain deep in my chest, and I pushed them away before they could take root. Anger was my go-to emotion, easy to slip into, requiring less thought. It was hateful at best and shameful at worst, but that didn't make it any less real.

It wore away at me, and it had only grown worse since Greg's death. I blamed him not only for what he'd become, but for what I'd become. I no longer recognized myself; I bore no resemblance to the self-assured young woman Greg had married. Over the years I'd gone from rowdy, to pensive, to downright reclusive. But we'd done it; we'd kept his secret. We'd shielded the kids, the coworkers, and the neighbors, Greg and I. At least there was that.

The *coup de grâce*? Greg had escaped and I was left to deal with the emptiness, not the emptiness that filled Greg's spot, but the emptiness that filled *me*. Self-pitying, no doubt, but as with the anger, that knowledge didn't make it any less real. I hated myself for the feelings I harbored, but admitting them seemed like something I needed to do. After all the years of deception, I craved honesty, even if that honesty was ugly.

I wish I could have been a better wife. I wish I could have given Greg the support he'd needed without nurturing a cold, hard knot of resentment. As I stood at the door, listening to the murmur of conversation coming from the porch, what I wished more than anything was that I could do as Erma said, that I could finally find my footing.

A tinkling laugh, the sound of cutlery, a soft sneeze, a muted, "Bless you." The breeze coming through the door was crisp but not cold, smelling of wet leaves and moist earth. I inhaled deeply, feeling more alive and aware than I had in years.

"Come on, child, and get you some lunch." Erma had looked up from her rocker and seen me standing at the door.

"We saved you plenty. That was a long walk you took this morning; I know you must be hungry."

I was, I realized, and pushed the door open to see a table laden with a tray of sandwiches, a bowl of what looked to be fresh-cut cantaloupe, and a pitcher of tea. My stomach growled at the sight. "I just wanted to apologize," I began, but Erma waved my words away.

"No need for that," she said. "Nothing to apologize for. Come join us, honey."

"Thank you, then," I tried again, but was again shushed.

"Stubborn one, aren't you? No need for thanks, either. Now have a seat."

Joseph Ammons rose from his chair to hold the door for me. "Take my seat," he said, gesturing. "I'm in need of a nap. I'm not as energetic as you young folk, you know." He winked, and I had to smile.

"He's right," said a voice with which I was unfamiliar, the words a bright, laughing melody. I peered around the door to see a tiny woman dressed in blue, her grey hair caught up in a bun. She was seated in the rocker against the house, facing Erma. "He's actually quite old compared to the rest of us. Especially me." She tucked a lock of hair back into the bun and rolled her eyes, smiling at me, a dimple showing amid the crease of her cheek. She was a weathered china doll of a woman with sparkling eyes and pink cheeks, and I liked her immediately.

"Emily Holt," said Erma, waving toward me, "this is my friend Corinne Johnson. Corinne, Emily. Corinne's husband used to own the repair shop, before he passed." She speared a piece of cantaloupe from the bowl. "Now sit down and eat, Emily, before the flies come out. It's only a matter of time, after a rain like that."

I thanked Joseph for holding the door before occupying a seat across from the two women and reaching for a sandwich. "The tea is sweet," Erma said, reaching for the pitcher. "That's how most of us drink it, but if you don't like it that way, I've got some lemonade in the kitchen."

"Sweet is perfect," I said, although I'd never had a glass of sweet tea in my life. Turns out I was right; the tea was heavenly: cold, soothing and delicious. Why had I never had this before? The women conversed around me as I ate; I was only vaguely aware of their voices dipping, rising, an occasional laugh. I was glad they didn't attempt to include me in the conversation. I was content just to sit, a part of, but with nothing expected from me.

A frog spoke up from somewhere close, maybe hidden in the rhododendrons. A trickle of rainwater continued through the gutter as lazy drips from the trees periodically spattered the roof. The sun, nearly overhead now, shone warmly on my right side, making me drowsy.

I was a child of the mountains, though my mountains were quite different from these. The Rockies were stark and brilliant, uncompromising and straightforward, even harsh in some ways, although breathtakingly beautiful. These mountains, in contrast, were lush and soft, bursting with life, assaulting the senses, beautiful in their own right. I'd missed mountains; it had taken me a long time to appreciate the different sort of flatland beauty Florida offered.

"Thank you for the lunch, Erma. I need all the energy I can get." Corinne Johnson's melodic voice penetrated through my thoughts. "I'm doin' crafts up at the lodge this afternoon. Jessie's flyin' in, too, did you know?"

"I'd heard from Kay she might be," Erma answered. "You tell her to come by and see me. Is Michael coming, too?"

"Not this time," Corinne answered, "but Jessie said we can plan on seein' him soon. She wouldn't tell me any more than that. You know Jessie; she's just like her momma when she wants to be. Won't tell nobody nothin'."

I hated to interrupt, but I wanted to know. "Is this the same Jessie who owns the lodge?"

"One and the same," said Corinne, and I could have sworn she had a note of pride in her voice. "She owns the mountain, too."

"Goodness," I replied, taken aback at the news. Cedar Hollow wasn't exactly a thriving metropolis; the thought there could be so much wealth in the tiny village surprised me. "The whole mountain? She obviously comes from money, then." The women didn't answer, just exchanged a smile they no doubt thought I missed. "There's something about that mountain," I continued, ignoring their look. "I'd still like to visit it. I can see it from my window. It was beautiful last night, with the lights on top. Peaceful, for some reason."

"Honey, that's not the lights makin' it peaceful." Corinne shook her head with a smile, and although the dimple was visible again, I detected a hint of sadness about her. I'd become an expert at detecting moods; it was second nature to me. "That's Billy May," Corinne was saying. "Jessie's momma. It's her spirit makin' it peaceful."

I was quickly growing accustomed to the locals' propensity for throwing out names as if I were supposed to know all about the person discussed. I was curious, but given Corinne's apparent sadness, it seemed rude to ask too much. Before I could decide whether to pursue my curiosity, Erma sat forward and addressed Corinne.

"Corinne, I never knew Billy May when she was a young girl. I first came to look at this house in the late spring of forty-six. Sue Ann Leary—Sue Ann Temple she was at that time, just recently widowed," Erma said, "was selling the house because Dr. Leary had passed on. Dr. Leary was her daddy"—this last part was spoken to me—"and by the time our business was finished and I moved in, the holiday season was nearly on us. Billy May was already gone by then, wasn't she?"

Corinne nodded, pursing her lips for a moment before answering. "She left a couple of months before you first came to see the house, Erma. Late winter, early spring, just after John Paul—John Paul was my husband," she said to me. "Just after John Paul and those others got back from the war. It was ..." She paused, watching a squirrel run along the branches of the old elm that took up much of the front lawn, " ... a bad time. A real bad time. After it ... after everything, she just plumb disappeared. Didn't a one of us know where she'd gone, not for years." Corinne looked down at her lap, gripping her hands so tightly together the knuckles had turned white.

Erma reached over to pat Corinne's locked hands. "She was a fine woman," she said. "I know you were close to her."

Corinne sniffled, producing a Kleenex from the front pocket of her skirt. "Yes, she was. And yes, I was. Since we was girls." She dabbed at her eyes. "You'll have to excuse me, honey," she said to me. "I know the last thing you need to see is a sentimental old woman bawlin' her eyes out."

"Please don't worry about me," I responded. "I'm laughing one minute, bawling the next these days."

She looked closer at me, momentarily distracted from her Kleenex. "Could be the change, you know. It'll do that to you."

I laughed. "I think it's more likely just a spell of temporary insanity."

"Well, honey," she said. "That's exactly what the change is."

Erma chuckled. "Licorice," she said. "I used to melt it to make my tea. Works better than anything, I tell you. Helps with the hot flashes, too. 'Course nowadays you can buy licorice pills, but back then, all I had was the candy. It's a wonder I didn't become diabetic. Lord only knows what Mr. Smith thought, with me buying up all his licorice like I did. When Billy May took over the store, she used to sit and have a cup with me from time to time, but she was partial to cherry bark. Said it helped with the aches and pains, but I couldn't abide the taste."

"Billy May had a remedy for everything," said Corinne. "John Paul always said it was hoodoo, but I always found Billy May's potions to work better than Dr. Hayden's, though I wouldn't have told him that."

"Oh, he knew," said Erma. "Billy May used to give him witch hazel for his back troubles." The women laughed and I had to smile, trying to picture the mysterious Billy May with her secret potions.

"It was good she came back," said Erma. "When was that? Seventy-five?"

"That's right."

"Gone thirty years." Erma paused and gave her head a little shake as if thinking it over. "She had her reasons for leaving, and her reasons for coming back. She seemed right glad to be back, though, didn't she?"

"She did." Corinne smiled, patting at one last tear. "I don't believe she ever thought she'd have a child, and you know Jessie meant the world to her. I think she'd given up on people, too, at the time she left. I'm just so grateful she got the chance to see how much we loved her. The folks down here missed her somethin' terrible when she was gone, but of course she didn't know that for the longest time. Billy May had been a social girl, you know, always in the middle of things. For her to have been alone up on that mountain all those years ... Well, it pains me to think of it, even now."

"But it all worked out for her in the end, didn't it?"

"Yes, it did. She was so happy, runnin' that store, takin' care of Jessie. The happiest I'd ever seen her."

"You seemed right happy, too."

"Oh, I was," said Corinne, the smile growing even brighter. "It was so good to have her back. I thought I'd lost her forever."

"Just goes to show we never know how things'll turn out." Erma turned to me. "Emily, I'm about as old as God himself, but I don't pretend to be wise. I don't know all the answers; none of us does, but you've managed to land yourself in a town full of old folks. You'd better get used to hearing advice, or at least opinions, and that's a fact. I suspect you've already figured that out by now."

I was so caught up in their story of Billy May's mysterious disappearance I jumped when Erma said my name. "Fire away," I said, delighted by her candor. She was right; I had managed to land in a town full of old folks, and I was already realizing they were an opinionated bunch. It didn't bother me; the opinions were offered with kindness, from what I'd so far seen. Who knew? Maybe I'd learn something, and even if I didn't, I was sure to be entertained.

"I can tell you this." Erma pointed a finger at me. "Life has a way of working itself out if you don't give up on it. Billy May didn't give up, and look how it turned out for her."

I wondered exactly how it *had* turned out for Billy May. Erma seemed to have forgotten I didn't know.

"Might not be exactly the way you thought it was going to be," Erma continued, "but that doesn't have to mean it's not good in its own way."

"That's right," Corinne piped up, sitting straighter and pushing with a foot to set her chair rocking. "Parts of my life turned out exactly the way I thought they would. Other parts was nothin' at all like what I expected. I can say without a doubt the same was true for Billy May. I reckon it's probably true for most all of us. I don't know that any of us end up with exactly the life we'd planned, but that doesn't mean there aren't good parts, all the same."

"I know that's right," said Erma, setting her glass on the table with a bang, causing the dishes to clatter and a bubble of laugher to work its way from my throat. "You speak the truth."

"What about you, Miss Erma Puckett?" Corinne asked, and the atmosphere lightened with her teasing tone. "How are things with ..." She left the question dangling, raising her brows and tilting her head toward the door.

Erma chuckled. "I guess you could rightly say that's another example of life working its way out in its own good time. And that's about all I have to say about that."

Erma and Joseph? I'd completely missed that one. I was learning a lot, sitting quietly, listening to those two old women talk. *Little pitchers have big ears.* I found myself remembering the idiom my grandmother used to quote when she'd catch me straining to hear adult conversations. Apparently, big pitchers do, too.

Joseph appeared in the door at that moment, eyebrows raised. "You ladies doing okay out here?"

"Did we disturb you, Joseph?" Erma asked. "I'm sorry."

"No, no. Not at all. It's these old bones," he said. "They yell at me when I'm not lying down, then they yell at me when I am. All the rain isn't helping much with that, I'm afraid."

Erma struggled to stand. "Did you use the liniment? It's in the medicine cabinet. Come on, honey, let's get you some help for those old bones."

Erma and Joseph, I thought again. Well, I'll be darned.

Chapter 16: Noah Holt

I woke up to the sound of Zach snoring, and it was such a familiar way to wake up it took me a minute to realize I was no longer twelve years old, I no longer had a skateboard, and I did, in fact, survive my first kiss with Jenny Higgins—and a few more after that. Then I remembered my mother was missing.

Sitting up, I banged my head on the ceiling, causing crumbs from the popcorn finish to rain down on my bed. I was also, I remembered, too tall to sleep on the top of a set of bunks. I brushed the powdery crumbs from my hair (my mother had always hated that finish, I remembered) and patted my pocket in search of my phone before realizing I'd left it charging by the outlet next to my mother's desk. "Just leave it," Zach had said. "I've got mine if anyone important calls." Apparently no one had, as neither Zach nor I had been awakened by the ringing of his phone.

Judging by the brightness shining around the window blinds, I guessed that it was midafternoon. The realization initially made me anxious, as if I'd missed something, or as if I had something important I was supposed to be doing. But the reality was, I had no idea what to do.

I lay back down and tried to come up with a mental list. Call Mom again and hope for an answer. Call the officer who'd taken my report and see if he had any news to share. Call all the numbers in Mom's appointment book to see if they knew where she was. I hated to admit it, but my mom didn't really have any close friends. I'd always thought that was weird, since her accounts of pre-married life were full of stories about partying with friends. She even had boxes of pictures to back up the stories, but I'd never seen her do more than chat over the fence with neighbors or volunteer with other parents on the PTA. She'd always gotten along well with everyone; she just hadn't extended the friendships any further than she'd needed to. After our discovery of the night before, I finally understood why.

Mom didn't even have any relatives, not since her parents had died, other than a second cousin or two in Colorado whose faces I wouldn't have recognized. Regardless, I made a note to call them, just in case. I couldn't think of anything else we could do to find her. I hoped Zach would have better ideas.

As heartless as it seemed to even think of it, and as much as I'd tried to put it out of my mind, Zach and I still had final exams to consider. It seemed a little ridiculous to worry about school given our current situation. Still, it didn't make sense to throw away a semester of work and wreck our GPAs; that wasn't going to do anybody any good.

I sat up again, more slowly this time, taking care with my head, and swung my legs over the side of the bed. When we were kids, Zach and I had made a game of jumping from the top bunk, measuring not only the vertical, but the horizontal distance traveled. Hearing the thumps and bangs my mother would come running, shouting at us to stop it before we broke our necks. We didn't stop, of course; we just piled pillows on the floor to muffle the sound. Smiling at the memory, I slid from the mattress, dropping the last six inches to the floor. As children, that drop had seemed enormous. I was beginning to understand that many things from my childhood hadn't been quite as they'd seemed.

Taking care not to wake Zach, I rummaged through my old chest-of-drawers for a change of clothes, then tiptoed from the room and softly closed the door. I wasn't quite sure of my plan at that moment, but I knew I needed a quick shower to clear the cobwebs from my brain. I felt gritty and dull; the past twenty-four hours had been a whirlwind of activity and emotion and had left me numb, unsure of my next move.

Stripping out of my clothes, I set the water to *cold* and stepped in, pulling the curtain closed behind me. *Noah, you're using up all the hot water*, my mother's voice played through my mind. *You boys are going to have to start paying the water bill if you keep taking hour-long showers.* It was true. Zach and I had taken such long, hot showers my mother had been forced to spray the ceiling with bleach, the bathroom fan no match for the spreading mildew of a hot, Florida summer.

She'd be pleased now, I thought, as I shivered under the showerhead, rinsing shampoo from my hair. It had worked; my brain was definitely clipping along better than it had been pre-shower. I scrubbed some warmth into myself with the towel and dressed quickly. I'd start by texting my professors. I felt sure once they knew my circumstances they'd work with me to get my finals completed in time. I needed to tie up that loose end in order to focus on the search for my mother without nagging distractions. After that, I'd go through her address book.

Detouring through the kitchen in search of caffeine and a snack, I paused at the window over the sink. It looked out on the fenced backyard, which, years ago, had contained a swing set, sandbox, and clubhouse. Our yard had been the one kids came to play in. I hadn't appreciated it then, of course; I guess kids never really do. My mother had been the one bringing us cookies and juice, the one bandaging skinned knees and providing ice for bumps and bruises. In many ways, my mother had been like one of us. Water balloon fights, games of hide-and-seek in the dark, roasted marshmallows over the fire pit; Mom had been a part of all of it. Our backyard was full of fun back then.

Our house, too, except when Dad was home. "Hold it down," Mom would say. "Your dad's working. He can't be disturbed." It was simply a part of our routine. Quiet when he was home, noisy when he wasn't. Dad would go on a business trip, and we'd have a sleepover. If I'd thought about it at all back then, I'd assumed it was Mom's way of distracting us from Dad's absence while at the same time allowing us to bring the pandemonium inside without fear of disturbing Dad's work.

The swing set and other outside toys had long since been torn down and replaced with planters. My mother loved to work in the yard, and her absence was noticeable. The crepe myrtle wasn't blooming and the jasmine was growing over the fence in a tangled mess. I'd fix that for her, I decided. I'd sprinkle bone meal around the crepe myrtle. I'd trim the jasmine and mow the yard and weed the planters. I'd make everything so perfect she'd want to come back home.

That thought bothered me. Somehow, beneath all the worry, fear, and uncertainty, I think a part of me knew my mother had run away. She'd broken free of what I'd previously thought was a comfortable suburban life, but was just coming to realize was, for my mother, a prison of sorts. I have to admit, the thought stung a bit. She had always seemed to love us, to *enjoy* us, even, but were we the ones responsible for keeping her in a place she didn't want to be? Would she have left him, had she not had us?

In running away from her previous life, wasn't she also running away from me?

No longer hungry, I grabbed a soda from the fridge and made my way to the office in search of my phone. Dropping into the desk chair I unplugged the phone from the charger and saw I'd missed a call from a number I didn't recognize, area code 304. Whoever they were, they'd left a message, but it would have to wait. The last time I'd received a message from a number I didn't recognize it had been a recording of someone trying to sell me Italian boots, "made from the finest leather." I wasn't in the mood for dealing with uninvited sales calls. I had more important things to do.

Chapter 17: Emily Holt

The afternoon was quiet, Erma having retired for a nap after our interesting lunch. I offered to clean up the dishes and wipe down the kitchen, and she thanked me with, I thought, some relief. After having his own nap interrupted, Joseph had apparently given up. Instead, he'd announced a trip to the grocery, written down a few requests Erma had made, and set off for Mr. Smith's. Corinne Johnson had welcomed me to town one more time before standing and preparing to leave for her craft session at the children's lodge.

"You know," she'd said from the bottom of the steps, "we had some good conversation, and what we said is true. Ain't a one of us hasn't had to start over from time to time. Startin' over ain't necessarily a bad thing. Sometimes, it's the best thing."

"Yes, ma'am," I answered her. "I know. I just haven't quite figured out how to get off the old path, or where I want the new one to go." I'd answered somewhat flippantly; the earlier gravity of their conversation had left me at loose ends. I wasn't ready for such serious introspection.

"Well, now, that can be a problem," she said, "but I have a feelin' you'll get it figured out pretty soon. Most of us do, eventually. We don't have much choice, do we? Otherwise we'd stay stuck on a path that don't go nowhere, and that's no way to live."

She was right; that was definitely no way to live. I'd been on a path going nowhere for a long time, especially since my boys left home. "I think it's regret," I blurted out, surprising myself. "And guilt. It doesn't feel right to start a new path when I've done such a terrible job on the old one. I don't seem to be much of a trailblazer. At least, not a good one."

Corinne turned her face toward the mountain in the distance, squinting in the sun. The slight breeze blew loose strands of hair around her face, and she reached to tuck one back into the low bun she wore. She was really quite beautiful, and I found myself wondering about the young woman she'd once been. "Regret and guilt," she said, and the tinkling note was gone from her voice. "Those are feelin's I know well." She turned back to me. "I'm eighty-two years old. Did you know that?"

I shook my head.

"Eighty-two," she repeated softly. "And I've lived sixty-seven of those years with the most soul-eatin' guilt you can imagine." She looked hard at me; then, apparently satisfied she had my attention, continued. "Traveled a lot of paths durin' that time, too. The regret came with me on every single one of 'em. It ain't somethin' you leave behind."

My heart dropped; I felt it as a physical sensation within my chest. I was dismayed by her words. "That sounds so hopeless," I said. "I'm sorry for whatever you went through; it must have been terrible, but how can you do that? How can you live with regret forever? I don't want the rest of my life to be filled with guilt."

"I didn't have much choice, and neither will you," she answered. "Some things can't be fixed. Oh, I know the experts will tell you different," she said, noticing my expression, "and I am most certainly not an expert. But it seems to me if you've done somethin' you regret, somethin' that changed the whole course of a life, either yours or someone you loved, you wouldn't want to forget it, not completely. You'd want to remember it so you don't never do it again. Remember it, and make amends. That won't fix it, but it'll keep you from doin' it again." She shifted her weight, leaning against the bannister for support.

"I can tell you this: I'm a better person because of the mistakes I've made. That don't mean I forget 'em. That don't mean I don't still live every single day of my life with regret. But I am a better person. I'm kinder; I pay more attention. I think about how what I do and say will affect somebody else, how it can hurt 'em or help 'em, dependin'. That's somethin', anyway. Somethin' more'n I did when I was young." She looked back toward the mountain, Billy May's mountain, I now knew, and I wondered at its significance for her. "You can't fix it, no. You can only say you're sorry and try to live a better life. That's all you can do."

"But what if the person I need to say it to is dead?" I asked, a note of frustration in my voice. This conversation wasn't exactly filling me with hope for my future. "It's too late to apologize."

"Then you say it to 'em dead," she said, looking at me and smacking the bannister for emphasis. "I do it every single day. What makes you think they can't hear you just because they're dead? That's just silly thinkin', right there."

The fervor with which she spoke both surprised and amused me. "What if they don't forgive?" I asked. It was a serious question, in spite of my amusement. I couldn't imagine Gregory forgiving me. I'd been the strong, capable one. My job had been to offer emotional support and fortitude. My breach of that unspoken contract would have been, I knew, unforgivable to Greg, or at least to the man he'd become.

"It ain't about forgivin'," said Corinne, "it's about bein' sorry for what you done, and livin' the rest of your life tryin' to make it right. If they forgive, well, that's an added bonus. But that ain't what it's about. You ain't supposed to be thinkin' about what they can do for you; you're supposed to be thinkin' about what you can do for them."

I understood what she was saying, and I didn't disagree, but there was a part of me that wanted absolution from Greg. I wasn't sure I could move forward without it. "What about you?" I asked. "Did they forgive you? This person you apologize to every day?"

Her features softened. "Billy May? Oh, she forgave me years ago, before you was even born. But I had a lot of makin' up to do. Still do." She glanced at the watch dangling loosely on her thin wrist. "And now I really do have to be goin'. Nice talkin' with you, honey." With one last wave she was off, hobbling down the street at a much faster pace than I'd have imagined her capable.

For the time being I was alone, kept company by my thoughts and the humming of the old refrigerator while I wiped down counters and washed the few dishes from our lunch. As I stacked saucers in the drainer to dry I was again reminded of my grandmother's house, and I was grateful for the accompanying feeling of security. The smell of lemon-scented dish soap, the chipped porcelain sink, the periodic creaks from the old house settling.

The feeling only intensified when I reached for the dish-towel hanging on a small hook to the side of the sink and realized it was a calendar towel, the year 1977, the dates surrounded by a border of pumpkins, squash, and other signs of a bountiful harvest. My grandmother's kitchen drawer had been full of such towels, dating all the way back to 1958, a beautiful calendar topped with a seasonal picture for each month. My favorite picture had been the one for May, a butterfly patterned with a kaleidoscope of colors.

I'd helped with the S&H trading stamps, the ones that could turn your tongue green if you licked too many in a sitting. My grandmother collected them from the grocery store, saving them in a kitchen drawer until she had enough to fill a book. She and I pasted them in her little booklets a couple of times each year, all the while discussing the items for which we might redeem them. One year a toaster, the next a lamp, but every year, a calendar towel. I hadn't thought of those towels in years.

They would have burned, of course, along with everything else from my grandmother's house. Faulty wiring, they said when it was all over. Thankfully, my grandmother was unharmed, but she had neither the means nor the energy to rebuild, and so moved in with my parents and me until she passed away a year later. I was a teenager at the time, more into record albums and stolen cigarettes than old calendar towels and lemon-scented kitchens.

I was too self-absorbed at that age to put much thought into what it must have been like for her. My grandfather, her husband, had died of a stroke before I was born. She'd outlived her husband, her home, and her independence. In many ways, she'd also lost her granddaughter, because I was much too busy with friends to take time to sit with her and work a puzzle or read a book. In my mind and my heart I'd loved her as much as always, but I'm certain I hadn't shown it. *I'm sorry, Grandma*, I said in my mind. Maybe Corinne was right; maybe my grandmother would hear my apology. It couldn't hurt to try.

Greg, however, would have to wait for another day. My feelings toward him were too complicated to tackle just then, the line between remorse and anger too undefined.

I put the last saucer in the china cabinet and rearranged the towel on its hook, then stood still for a moment, absorbing the stillness emanated by Erma's kitchen. The boys and I were the last of my family, at least of the direct line. My parents died within a month of one another the year Zach left for college, and I'd had no siblings. It was tough to lose my parents, not only for the obvious reasons, but also because they were the only ones in whom I'd ever confided the true state of my family. When they were gone, I had no one.

I wandered through the boarding home lost in thought, straightening a pillow here, moving a knickknack there, rearranging flowers, angling furniture. Vines and Roses was an exquisite place; my meddling was in no way intended to mean otherwise. I'd always dealt with stress by fidgeting, moving furniture, repositioning artwork. It was soothing to me. In my worst moments, I'd painted walls and tiled floors. During one particularly stressful time, I'd knocked out a non-load-bearing wall and created a rec room—or a wreck room, as my father had teased.

I was restless, agitated, full of pent-up energy. I hadn't yet heard back from the boys, and although I knew they were busy, I found I had a great deal of things I wanted to share with them. Things about their father, about our family history, even things about the strange town of Cedar Hollow. If I hadn't heard from either of them by dinnertime, I decided, I'd call again.

The thought of dinner sparked an idea, one that once acknowledged, refused to leave. I hadn't yet visited the diner, "Kay's place," as everyone kept saying, although the name on the sign out front clearly advertised *Peggy's Diner*, yet another anomaly of the town. I'd pay a visit, I decided, and while there, pick up dinner for Erma, Joseph, and Geraldine. I had the funds; that wasn't an issue. Besides, I was growing to appreciate these elderly folks who'd taken such an interest in me.

Mobilized by my idea, I quickly checked my reflection in the entryway mirror—flushed, but not too bad—and let myself out, relishing the cool breeze against my face as I headed to the center of town.

Chapter 18: Kay Langley

"**I** don't much care for that one, Riva. It's too ... what's the word I'm lookin' for? Citified."

Riva laughed at my description. "No, I'm not too fond of that one, either. But look at this one." She pulled out another swatch of fabric, this one decorated with tiny salt and pepper shakers. "We might be able to stitch up some right cute curtains with this one, don't you think?"

I didn't want to hurt Riva's feelings, but I just couldn't picture any of her samples looking right in my diner. I wasn't sure how to describe what was wrong with them. They were cute enough; they just weren't right.

We both looked up at the bell to see a woman who could only be Erma's latest guest from the boarding home. It wasn't too hard to figure that out; after all, we knew everyone else in town. She didn't look crazy, I was a little relieved to see. She looked just fine. A small woman dressed in jeans, dark, curly hair twisted in a loose bun, face clean of makeup. It was hard to picture her laughing hysterically from the floor of Mr. Smith's General Store. Then again, it was hard to picture a whole heck of a lot of the folks in Cedar Hollow doing things we all knew they'd done, myself included.

"Hi," she said, giving us a little wave. It was our slow time of day, between lunch and dinner, and she was the only customer.

"Take a seat anywhere you like," Riva said to her, pushing the sample materials aside.

"Actually, I'm just stopping in to ask if you do carryout," she said, approaching the bar. "I was hoping to buy dinner for the people at Vines and Roses. They've been so good to me, in spite of all the trouble I must be." She slid onto a stool and smiled. "I'm afraid I seem to bring chaos wherever I go. I'm Emily," she said, reaching a hand across the counter. "Emily Holt."

There was something immediately likable about the woman. Maybe it was her quick smile, or maybe just that she came across as an ordinary woman, down-to-earth with a sense of humor about herself. Now that I'd met her, I had to agree with Erma. She wasn't a criminal. At that point, I wasn't even sure she was crazy.

"Nice to meet you, Emily," I said, shaking her hand. "That's my daughter's name. I'm Kay Langley, owner of this fine establishment, and this here is Riva, my manager."

Riva pulled a face at my description of her. "Manager, is it now? I must have gotten a promotion. How do, honey. To answer your question, we do carryout, carry-in, delivery, special order; you name it, we do it, and that's a mighty nice thing for you to do for Erma. What did you have in mind?"

"I was hoping you all could help me with that," she said. "I'm guessing you ladies probably know what everyone in town likes to eat."

I laughed; she was sure enough right about that.

"I'll need plates for Erma, Joseph, and Geraldine," she said. "And me, too, I guess. I'd love a big chef salad, but what would they like?"

That was easy. "Pot roast for Joseph," I said. "Chicken and dumplin's for Geraldine. And Erma won't eat more'n cereal for her last meal of the day, maybe with some fruit on the side. She won't want anything heavy that late, says it interferes with her sleep. Do you want to stay and get it now so you can warm up what needs warmin' this evenin', or do you want Hannah—Hannah's my granddaughter—to deliver it to you this afternoon fresh?"

"What's the least amount of trouble for you?" she asked, winning herself a place in my heart. When was the last time a customer had asked me that question? I love each and every one of my customers, have known most of them my whole entire life, but I'm generally the one taking care of them, not the other way around. That's as it should be, of course, but still, I was touched by her concern.

"None of it is any trouble at all, honey, but food is always better fresh. Why don't you plan on Hannah bringin' it around five o'clock? Andrew'll have everything ready by then. Are you sure there isn't anything we can get for you now? Coffee? Pie?"

"Now that you mention it, coffee sounds good," she said. "I started out the day with a lot of energy, but circumstances seem to have drained it out of me."

I had to work to keep my face straight. As I've said before and will no doubt say again, Cedar Hollow is a small town. Nothing happens in this town that don't make its way back into my diner. This time, it had been William, from over at the train station, who'd been driving by on his way to us for lunch when he'd seen the sheriff helping a muddy Mrs. Holt from his patrol car. I reckoned she *was* tired, after a morning like that, whatever *that* had been.

"Coffee it is," I said, managing to hide my smile. "Riva, you might want to move this stuff before it gets spilled on. We'll figure all this out, later. Riva wants to fix up the place," I said by way of explanation. "And I know we need to. Just can't figure out how to do it, is all."

At those words, Emily Holt perked right up. "Would you mind if I look at those?" she asked. "Back in the day, I used to do some decorating. Then I got married, had kids, you know how it is."

I didn't know how it was, exactly, because I'd been a part of the diner since before I could walk. That didn't stop with marriage and kids; I just worked them right into the diner along with me. Still, I know enough to realize not everyone has been as lucky as I have, and Emily Holt's experiences were clearly different from mine.

"Don't mind at all," I said. "Riva, slide 'em over to her. Now, honey, I've got some coffeecake here I'm about to have to throw out if you don't help me eat it. Just a little piece? It's not the freshest by now, but it's on the house."

"I shouldn't," she said with a sigh, "but I will. Thank you. So this material"—she spread the swatches on the bar in front of her—"is it for curtains?"

"It's supposed to be," I answered, "but I can't figure out exactly what I want." I set a slice of cake and a fork in front of her and leaned over to look. "None of these seem quite right. Do they, Riva? What do you think?"

"No, I agree," Riva said, to my relief. "It's hard to know what to do with a place when it's looked exactly the same for fifty years."

"More'n that, except for the curtains momma hung back when I was pregnant with Emily," I said. "Just about everything else is as I remember it from childhood, just the way my grandmomma had it."

"Some of these are cute," said Emily. "Salt and pepper shakers, fruits and vegetables, forks and spoons." She held a couple of the pieces of cloth up for inspection. "But to be honest, I think that's the problem."

"What do you mean?" I pulled a stool up behind the counter and took a seat. I was curious to see what this woman had to say.

"I mean, when you think of this place, your diner, do you think of 'cute'?"

I shook my head. "No, I can't say that's the word that comes to mind. We're just ordinary, hard-workin' folks. People come here to get a good meal and visit with neighbors. Peggy's Diner is the meetin' spot for the town. If you want to know how Darryl Lane's hip surgery went, or how the remodel down at the school is goin', or even when the next fish supper over at the church is happenin' you come here and somebody will know the answers."

"So it's comfortable," she said. "Inviting. Authentic."

"Those words would work, don't you think, Riva?"

"Absolutely. And I'll add 'homey' to the mix. The diner is like a second home to people around here."

"Then that's what you want it to reflect," said Emily. "You don't want a gimmick."

"That's right," I said. She was doing a good job explaining what I hadn't known how to explain. "You know how some restaurants all have the same look? I don't want that. We're not a chain; we're a real place with real history."

"You want a look that's true to the town. A look that shows the history of the place, but not just a cute idea of what that history might look like."

"Exactly," said Riva, and I could tell she was getting excited by the notion.

"Then you want burlap," said Emily, just like that. "Not curtains, though. Valances. Burlap valances with a gingham trim. Whatever color you choose for the gingham will decide the colors you use throughout. Red gingham, red accents. Are you going to reupholster?" She looked around the diner and I have to admit, seeing it through her eyes, I was embarrassed by how raggedy it had all become.

Why, one of the seats in a back booth, the one against the wall to the left, even had duct tape holding the vinyl together. It had been that way for over a year, maybe even two, ever since Richard Huffman, the caretaker up at the children's lodge, accidentally sat on his big old ring of keys and punctured through the seat. He and his wife, Opal, felt terrible about it. They offered to pay to have it recovered, but it was so old, anyway, recovering it in something new would have made it stand out too much from the rest. Besides, the Huffmans had become good friends over the past few years. More than once they'd jumped in to help me when an unexpected crowd was more than Riva and I could handle. No way in the world was I going to let them pay to fix that seat, but I sure was hoping Emily Holt couldn't see it from her stool at the bar.

"Yes, we are," I said, having just made up my mind. Beside me, Riva squealed, but I refused to look at her. Given the way I'd been raised, knowing life can turn hard without a minute's notice, I'd always been careful with my money. "Kay'll pinch a penny so hard it screams," my late husband used to tease, but maybe it was time to let some of those screaming pennies go. I don't like to think too far ahead, but the reality of the situation is that one day the diner will belong to Andrew, and I don't want to leave a mess behind for him to have to fix up. I don't like change, never have, but I was willing to listen to whatever ideas Emily had, so long as she didn't try to turn my diner into something it wasn't meant to be.

"In that case, I'd suggest red gingham and ecru upholstery," she was saying. "The ecru will match the burlap and emphasize the simple, understated look you want, but the red will give the place some color. You can accent with red gingham napkins or red picture frames. There are all sorts of ways to work it."

Riva and I looked at each other. I would have never thought of making curtains out of burlap—goodness sakes, burlap was for potato sacks—but as soon as she said it, I knew it was right.

"Burlap and gingham," said Riva. "Who would have thought? Back when we was kids, you'd have had to be the poorest of the poor to wear burlap. I don't think the Pritchetts even wore burlap, did they Kay?" She didn't wait for me to answer. "Maybe they did, now that I think of it. Old Junior, anyway, for his shirts. Now, flour sacks," she said, "that was somethin' different. Most all of us wore flour sacks in one way or another, either as a skirt or an apron, or what have you. Feed sacks, too, 'cause they was cotton. I know I did, and I know you did, too, Kay. But burlap?" Riva laughed. "It just struck me how crazy it is that those of us in flour sacks looked down on those in potato sacks. Lord have mercy, like a one of us was any better than any other. All of us was so poor we barely had a pot ... Well, you know. I don't want to offend our out-of-town guest."

She was right with her memories. I suppose no matter how big or how small a place is, there will always be those looking to prove they're better than the other, even if the only difference is potato burlap against flour cotton.

"It sounds crazy," Riva was saying, "but I can see it. Can't you, Kay?" I nodded at her, but she didn't give me a chance to speak before she went on. "I think it might actually work. I don't know about 'ecru,' though. What exactly is it?"

I didn't know either, and I was glad she had asked.

"It's in the brown family," Emily said. "Kind of beige, but darker. It's a good color for upholstery because it's light enough not to darken the place, but dark enough not to show dirt. May I see your pen?"

Well, I had sure learned something new. I handed Emily my pen and she pulled a napkin out of the canister and began drawing. "Like this. See how it comes together? Or, you could do this." The pen flew over the napkin. "This is an option, too, but it's not my favorite. I like this one best." She set down the pen and looked at us.

This woman was an artist. That was plain to see, but I admit I was purely surprised at that fact. Given the way Hannah had said she was dressed when she came to town, I wouldn't have pegged her as someone with the artistic eye, so to speak. But what she'd drawn was exactly what I would have pictured for my diner if I'd had the ability to describe what I was looking for. Riva was just as impressed. I could tell by the way she kept poking me in the ribs.

Before I could comment on what Emily was showing us, the white van from the children's lodge pulled up to the front door. "The kids are here," I told Riva. "I was hopin' they'd come by today. Emily?"

She looked up from her drawing. "Can you come back tomorrow around the same time?" I asked. "I'd like to hear more of your ideas."

"Absolutely." She smiled, looking as excited by the whole discussion as Riva did, but before I could remark on it little Robby O'Brien came flying through the door and practically threw himself into me, wrapping his arms around my waist. I do love that child. Robby is a local, one of us. I knew his grandparents, both passed on now, and I also know his momma, who I knew must be working for Dr. Poindexter for the day. Robby stays up at the lodge on the days his momma works.

"And there's Jessie, too," said Riva, nodding toward the door. "Goodness, they've got a van full of kids, don't they?

Let me get busy with some ice cream." She pulled bowls and spoons from the shelf as I squeezed Robby in a hug and Emily put a couple of bills on the bar, standing to leave.

"Looks like you guys are about to get overrun," she said. "I'll get out of your way."

"We are definitely about to get overrun," I agreed. "Sure you don't want to stay? This is the highpoint of our week, me and Riva. We love havin' the kids come by."

"Maybe next time," she said, "but I've got some more ideas I need to get down on paper. I have a memory like Swiss cheese these days. If it's not written down, it never happened."

"I know how that is, honey. I'd like to tell you it gets better with age, but that wouldn't be the truth. Hannah'll bring your dinner over at five. And do come back by tomorrow, all right? I'd like to see those ideas."

"I will, and thank you." She waved, dodging the incoming group of kids, wheelchairs, and staff. I watched her go, then held Robby away from me to get a good look at him. He was getting older, our boy. Still small for his age, still cute as ever, but even closer to eye-level than he'd been just the week before.

"How's my boy doin'?"

"Good, Mrs. Kay. Can I have vanilla this time?"

"You sure can." Robby has Down syndrome and sometimes has a hard time speaking his words just right, but Jessie had arranged for him to get all kinds of speech therapy up at the lodge, and I could already tell a difference. I'd have bet money his words were clearer than mine just then. "Hop up on a stool, and we'll get you fixed up with some vanilla."

"Good afternoon, Kay," Jessie called over the ruckus. "How've you been?"

"Doin' good, Jessie. You?"

"Absolutely wonderful." Jessie smiled, and it was a beautiful sight, not just because she was a beautiful woman, but because for a good long stretch of time—years, in fact—Jessie hadn't smiled at all.

"And I get to be the ring bearer," said Robby, stopping on his way around the counter to turn back to me with a grin. "I get to give them the rings."

It took me a minute to understand; I'll blame that on how distracted I was, given all the children and the noise. But when I did, I looked up at Jessie, the question on my face.

Her smile was as big as the sun, it really was, and I'd have given just about anything for Billy May to have seen her at that moment. She'd have been so happy for her baby girl. Jessie held up her left hand, wriggling the fingers at me, and I am not a sentimental sort, I truly am not, but I had to blink a couple of times to clear my eyes. It could have been due to the light reflecting off that stone on her finger, but it might not all have been. It might not have. I'm not ashamed to say it.

We have our hard times here in Cedar Hollow, but we have a way of pulling together to help each other out of them. My momma always said if you didn't have some hard times, you couldn't enjoy the good ones, and I reckon she was right. Billy May, more than any of us, knew that. She had a pure joy of the good times, the times before the mountain, and the times since she found Jessie. I wished more than anything Billy May could be sitting in my diner at that moment, but I also had a sneaking suspicion she was doing just that. A part of me really believes she was.

Chapter 19: Sheriff John Moore

I'd had a feeling about Emily Holt. A hunch, you might call it. In my line of work, you learn to pay attention to hunches. It was a hunch that probably saved Jessie McIntosh's life up at the children's lodge a couple of years ago. It was a hunch that saved the lives of seven of my men when Iraqi insurgents ambushed us back in '93, and a hunch of an entirely different sort that saved me from what would have undoubtedly been a terrible marriage in '95. More recently, a hunch had gotten me to the doctor in time to save my own life.

Then there are the times I should have listened, but didn't. Like September 15, 1991, the day my gut told me Boston College's tight end was going to go low. I should have listened to it, but I didn't, and I ended up with a blown-out ACL and a blown-up football career. I'd made a habit of listening since then.

Now, I had a hunch about Emily Holt. I hadn't asked for her license or registration because technically, I hadn't pulled her over. Instead, I'd happened upon her, as it were. And so far as I know the law—and I like to think I know it pretty damned well—it's not illegal to fall out of cars or slide down mountains, at least not in the state of West Virginia. Weird as hell, but not illegal, not even in any of our old, obsolete laws, and we've got some doozies.

For example, anytime a train runs within a mile of a community of a hundred people or more, the community has to build a station. That one goes a long way toward explaining why a little town like Cedar Hollow rates a train station. But don't fall asleep on that train; that's illegal. You can't legally whistle underwater—at least not for fun, and why the hell else would you be whistling underwater?— you can't legally swear in public, and you can't legally own a red flag, but by God, you can fall out of cars and slide down mountains all day long, if that's what you want to do.

Apparently, that was what Emily Holt wanted to do.

All of which made me curious. I didn't have her license or registration, but what I did have was her plate number. That was all I needed. It didn't take long to uncover a missing person's report, filed with the Orange Park Police Department outside of Jacksonville, Florida. The report was taken by Officer Rick Higgins.

No way in hell, I thought. I knew a Rick Higgins, or at least had at one time. Marine Corps Base Quantico, 1992. I graduated third in my class. Rick Higgins graduated first. Hell of a guy, Rick. I wondered at the chance of this Higgins being the same one.

"Festus!" he said by way of greeting when he finally came on the line.

Yep, same one. Festus was the limping deputy sheriff from the old television series *Gunsmoke*. I'd had the name bestowed upon me shortly after my arrival at Camp Pendleton, and despite my best efforts, it had followed me to Quantico. I'd lied to the recruiting officer, lied to the doctors, and lied to everyone in between, but there were some days the bum knee got the best of me, and try as I might, I couldn't completely hide that fact.

I wasn't a liar by nature, but when the hoped-for football career went south and I returned to the Pittsburgh suburb I'd grown up in, one thing was clear: I couldn't stay there. My stepfather was drinking as much as ever and my mother was still under his thumb. Me, though, I'd changed. The first time the old man came at me with a closed fist, I snapped his arm up behind his back and drove him to his knees. It was time to go, and a recruiting station downtown helped me leave.

"Einstein," I replied, using his old nickname. Damn, the man was smart. There's no doubt in my mind I'd have been a lot farther down the list than third if it hadn't been for Higgins.

"It's good to hear from you, man," he said. "I heard you'd gotten yourself elected sheriff out in the middle of nowhere. Is that true?" His Boston accent brought back memories of late nights spent pouring over regulations. *Think, Festus*, he used to say. *You know this shit. Just think for a minute.*

"It's true," I confirmed. "Wasn't a lot of competition."

He laughed. "Well, congratulations, anyway. So is this a work-related call, then?"

"'Fraid so," I answered, and nearly smiled. Neither of us had been much good at small talk. It was just like Higgins to jump straight to the point, another trait of his I appreciated. "I believe we've got a woman you've been looking for."

"Emily Holt," he said.

"That's the one."

"She been arrested?"

"No. No, nothing like that. She's taken a room at the boarding home here in town. Cedar Hollow," I clarified. "West Virginia," I clarified more. Many people as close as Huntington had never heard of Cedar Hollow. I was fairly certain no one in Jacksonville, Florida had.

"She okay, then?"

"Well," I hesitated. "She's in one piece, if that's what you mean."

"You read the report."

"I did. Possible mental health issues, you said. I don't think she's a danger to herself or anyone else. She's a little out there. A little strange. But nothing to take in front of a mental health commissioner. In my opinion, that is."

"Good. That's good. Lost her husband a year ago. Her kids got worried when they realized she'd taken off without telling them. They thought she might be having a hard time dealing with the anniversary of his death. All right, then," he said, all business. "I'll take care of things on this end."

"I'll go find Mrs. Holt and let her know her kids are worried. Shouldn't be too hard to find. Probably lying in a road somewhere."

"What? I thought you said she wasn't a danger." I could almost hear him sitting up straighter.

"She's not. I don't think she's trying to hurt herself. She just seems to like our asphalt."

"Well, all right, then. You said she was strange. That makes me believe it. Next time we talk, we need to catch up a little bit."

I agreed, and we disconnected.

I'd been serious when I stated Mrs. Holt should be easy to find. According to the sign at the entrance to town, 219 people called Cedar Hollow home. Anyone would be easy to find in Cedar Hollow. If she wasn't at the boarding home or the diner, I'd take Main Street to Deer Jump, and if experience was anything to go by, I'd find her there. Just hopefully not lying in the road.

Chapter 20: Emily Holt

The afternoon sun was warm, the only evidence of a morning storm the muddy trail and the moist, earthy smell of the land. I scooted up on the boulder and looked out over what I'd already begun to think of as my meadow, pulling my new red jacket around me in the cool breeze. The buttercups were no less brilliant than I remembered, butterflies and honeybees flitting among them in a pattern only they could understand. I'd known immediately where I needed to go to draw my sketches. There was something so tranquil, yet so simultaneously alive, about the little paddock.

I'd left the diner, dodging between kids and staff (one of whom, cleaned up a bit and glamorized, could have been a dead-ringer for movie producer Jessica McIntosh as she'd appeared on the Oscars back in March—I've always been a sucker for the Oscars), and checked in at the boarding home. Joseph was sitting on the front porch with a book in his lap. "No, no phone calls," he'd said at my query. "But if there is one, we'll be sure to let you know. Oh, before I forget, Erma laid a jacket out on your bed. Help yourself to it. I imagine it's a mite chilly here compared to Florida."

I didn't know where it came from, but I accepted it with gratitude, thrilled it was the right size, even more thrilled it was red. He was right; I'd been colder in the last twenty-four hours than I could remember being in the last twenty years, certainly since moving south from Colorado. The realization made me smile. When we'd first moved to Florida I'd enjoyed poking fun at our neighbors anytime the temperature dropped below seventy-five. Shivering, rushing from car to house, they'd call over to each other, remarking on the cold front. Let it drop below sixty and the hats and gloves came out, much to my amusement. I don't remember precisely when I became acclimated to the warmer weather, but my teeth had chattered so much in the past twenty-four hours, my jaws were tired.

Zipped up to my neck and grateful for the warmth, I'd next gone in search of art supplies, nothing fancy, just a tablet and some colored pencils. I'd quickly discovered in a town as small as Cedar Hollow, with the school year nearly over, art supplies were hard to come by.

Finally, situated comfortably on the boulder, I flipped open the composition book I'd uncovered on a dusty shelf in the back of Mr. Smith's General Store and uncapped my pen. My brain felt as if it were practically buzzing with ideas, a feeling I hadn't had in years and had long since forgotten. Forced myself to forget, actually, because remembering was too painful.

Within a week of Noah's birth, I'd come to understand my career was over. I could never leave the kids alone with Greg. Hell, I could never leave a babysitter alone with Greg. I didn't yet have the words to describe what was happening with him back then; *nervous breakdown* was the most fitting term, but even that didn't adequately describe his downward spiral. I'd never witnessed anything like it.

They were good babies, both of them, but Greg was unable to handle the upheaval that comes with having young children. He'd done fairly well when it was just Zach. If he'd left the bulk of the work to me, he'd at least paid attention to Zach, even composing a song he'd sing to him before bedtime. I hadn't thought of Greg as the most responsive of fathers, but neither had I thought of him in any sort of negative capacity, certainly not when it came to our baby. In fact, I'd found his singing sweet, even bragged about it to friends and clients. Not every baby is lucky enough to be the recipient of an original composition by Dad, after all.

But when there were two, it was too much for him. The crying, the sleepless nights, the endless energy of a two-year-old, all of it combined to send Greg over the fragile precipice of whatever mental stability he'd managed to accrue. He locked himself in the office for days, unshaven, unclean, his hands shaking nearly to the point of convulsions. He paced and muttered; he smacked himself in the head and hit walls until even I had to admit this was beyond the pale, something much deeper and more frightening than a poeticized artistic temperament.

He skipped out on gigs, ignored his bandmates' calls, and drank beer after beer until his sweat reeked of alcohol and yeast and the entire west end of our house smelled like a brewery. I did my best to hide the truth of our circumstances from friends and family, partly out of loyalty to Greg, partly out of embarrassment, but it became impossible to hide, not only because Greg's behavior was deteriorating, but because my own health was at risk. I was at the end of my rope, both physically and emotionally. I had a newborn and a toddler to care for. I had a fledgling career I was trying to keep afloat. And I had Greg, who was making everything else impossible.

When I stumbled into the office at the crack of dawn to find Greg naked, rocking to and fro in the corner of the room, I left him. I suppose I should have been afraid for him—not *of*, mind you, but *for*, and it's an important distinction not only because I was never afraid of Greg, but because often, when I should have been afraid *for* him, I failed the test. To be completely honest, I was too tired and pissed off that night, and many others, to register fear. To knock even more points off my perfect wife score, I was disgusted. There you have it. The truth, in all its terrible nakedness, no metaphors or puns intended.

I'd been up the entire night, first walking Noah to try to soothe his colic, then rocking Zachary, who couldn't understand why his baby brother screamed so much. Finally, after both boys were asleep and I stood in silence for the first time all night, swaying from fatigue, I realized I hadn't seen Greg for hours. Maybe even days. Who could say with any certainty? I'd completely lost track of time, going from feeding to bathing to walking and rocking with no breaks between. I opened the office door to see Greg's naked white ass pointed at me from the back corner and immediately closed it again.

I loaded both boys into the car, the two of them so worn out by then they didn't even awaken. I grabbed my purse and the cat, who scratched the living daylights out of me, backed out of the garage, and drove to my parents' house, where I remained for two months until Greg agreed to go for help. Well, I don't know if *agreed* is the right word. He didn't have much choice, once the police arrived and carted him off to the hospital.

Bipolar disorder, they said, severe, with psychotic features. I'll be honest; I'd never heard of it. Manic-depressive, they explained. Mood swings, from mania to depression, hence the *bi*. It sounded so simple. I'd originally termed Greg's odd behaviors mood swings, too, but this ... it was indescribable. Until you know, you don't know; it's impossible to explain, so much more complicated than the term implies.

A mood swing is when you're frustrated the alarm didn't go off, then happy you missed all the red lights, then annoyed when your coworker makes a sarcastic comment. *That's* a mood swing, and apparently, that's all many with the diagnosis experience, if to an advanced degree. That's what Greg initially experienced, too, a precursor, maybe, to what was to come. I could see it in hindsight, but I hadn't recognized it for what it was. None of us had.

In some ways, I think his mother struggled the most, because she blamed herself for missing something. *What*, she couldn't say, but surely *something*. We'd never been close, Mrs. Holt and I, but thrown together by our connection to Greg, we grew to lean on each other during the weeks of Greg's first hospitalization. First. Yes, there were more.

Mrs. Holt picked apart scenes from his childhood relentlessly, looking for clues. Was she too demanding? Too permissive? Too absent? Was it because of the divorce?

"He was spirited," she told me once, shortly after I'd moved back home that first time. Greg was still in the hospital, and Mrs. Holt had begun to spend more and more evenings at our house, as if immersing herself in Greg's material trappings might somehow lead to an understanding of what had gone wrong. "Nervous. He was an anxious little boy, always chewing on his fingernails or rocking in his seat." She rinsed the baby bottles she'd been washing and set them in the drainer to dry. "I'd fuss at him about it, telling him to get his dirty fingers out of his mouth, or quit rocking in the chair before he broke it. Emily, do you think that's—"

"No." I interrupted her, adjusting Noah in one arm to reach over and hug her with the other. "Stop that. It's nothing you did; it's nothing I did. It's nothing Greg, did, either; we need to remember that." I'd said *we*, but even then, I knew I meant *I*. Rationally, logically, I of course knew the illness was a separate entity from Greg, an alien invader that wormed its way into his brain and waged war against him. But when the invader wears the face of the loved one, it's sometimes hard to separate the two.

"Maybe if I'd gotten him help sooner?" his mother was asking. "Maybe if his father hadn't remarried? He had a hard time with that; he really did. He stayed locked in his room for weeks that summer, wouldn't even come out to eat. I had to take his dinner to him and stand over him to make sure he ate it. He was upset. Of course he was; we both were. He felt as if his father had thrown us away. Well, so did I, to tell you the truth, because that's exactly what he'd done. I tried to hide all that from Greg, but maybe he picked up on my thoughts anyway. I should have gotten help for him back then. If I had, maybe—"

"Hush," I told her, something I wouldn't have dared say only a few weeks before. "You couldn't have known. No one could have known. We could 'maybe' ourselves to death over this, but it wouldn't make any difference. Greg has always been moody. He's always been overly-sensitive, even a little paranoid, at least since I've known him. No one could have known it would lead to this."

While his mother picked apart her years with Greg in search of answers, I did the same with mine. Had I somehow triggered this in Greg? How did he go from moodiness to psychosis in the blink of an eye? What had I missed?

No one knew why things changed, not his many doctors over the years, not Greg himself, and certainly not me. But whether from the *severe* part or the *psychotic* part, mood swings couldn't even begin to describe the challenges Greg faced from that moment on. Or, for that matter, the challenges I faced because of him.

From the highest high, believing he was on the cusp of writing the most brilliant pop song ever, seeing nonexistent musical notes floating through the air and hearing sonatas emanating from the walls, to the lowest low, threatening to end his own life, and sometimes mine along with it. All of that, mixed with concurrent delusions, nonsensical thoughts, and a hefty dose of paranoia, just to make things interesting. *That's* what Greg experienced.

The name would continue to change slightly over the years, not because Greg changed, but because panels, committees, professionals, and insurance boards spent inordinate amounts of time trying to phrase it just right. Bipolar I—or was it II?—catatonic features, psychotic features, in partial remission ... mixed ... in full remission ... and on and on it went. If only they'd spent as much time trying to cure it as they did trying to name and bill for it, things may have turned out differently, or so I told myself. They could have called it Bat-Shit-Crazy Syndrome, for all I cared; I just needed them to *fix* it. Who cared about a label when our lives were crumbling all around us?

To add to our frustration—on this, Greg and I were fully aligned, and *frustration* is too simple a word to convey our full range of feelings—books and movies romanticized the disorder. Contrary to popular belief, mania isn't always full of profound insights and marvelous escapades. Greg wasn't skipping along rooftops, pirouetting in the wind, and solving complex equations. No, Greg's periods of mania included debilitating paranoia, delusions, and hallucinations, some of which, given the sheer number of episodes he had, may possibly have been profound, but who could tell? Most were simply heartbreaking and self-destructive. Some, a few, were even dangerous. So much for Hollywood glamorization.

But I didn't want to think about that. I wanted to think about burlap curtain panels with gingham trim. I wanted to think about ambiance, vintage furnishings, and wainscoting. It frustrated me that thoughts of Greg kept intruding. I'd lived the majority of my life reacting to Greg. Now that he was dead, why couldn't I leave him behind? Better yet, why couldn't he leave me alone?

I knew the answer to those questions, of course, but I wasn't ready to face them. I slid down from the boulder, leaving the notebook and pen behind, and walked over to squat beside the creek. The water was crystal clear, rushing its way down the mountain with the faint, musical sound of a wood-wind quartet. The thought amused me; I suppose it's impossible to live so many years with a musician without subtly changing the way one hears the world. The wind through treetops made the sound of brushes on a snare; the buzzing bees provided a soft bass, the cicada hidden somewhere in the underbrush an accompanying maraca.

Greg had once explained to me his belief that every sound on earth has the potential to be music, set within the proper composition. "That's the key, Em," he'd said, not in a manic moment, simply in a moment of passion for his craft. "The proper composition. You'll hear some people say every sound is music, but that's not true. Not any more than every word is a story. It takes putting those sounds into the proper composition to make music, just as it takes putting those words in the proper composition to make a story."

I loved listening to Greg when he was well. I loved the depth of feeling he had for his music, and I admired the wealth of knowledge he demonstrated. It was a large part of what had drawn me to him in the first place. In spite of everything, Greg really was a brilliant musician. Life had been unfair to him. It was sometimes hard to look past my own resentments to remember Greg was the true victim. His illness robbed me of a normal life, rendering me little more than a shadow in his life story, but it robbed him of *himself*, which must have been infinitely worse.

To be fair, there were calm periods, too. He wasn't always sick, or at least not to an extent anyone other than I would have recognized. He had long periods during which a combination of medication and circumstances kept him stable. The problem, for me at least, was that I'd lost trust. After that first episode, I never again saw Greg as truly whole. He was fragile, unpredictable, unreliable. It didn't matter how long he was able to maintain stability—he once went for over three years without a single issue—I didn't trust it. I remained alert, watching and waiting and placating and doing everything in my power to *hold it together*, the *it* being our family, our lives. Greg.

How could I not, after what I'd witnessed? I never again trusted that whatever Greg felt during any given moment was normal. Was he a little too energetic? Was he overreacting? Had his sleep patterns changed? I put him in an unwinnable situation; I realize that. Greg couldn't experience the minutest of mood changes without me hovering over him, asking if he was sure he felt all right. I couldn't help myself. Not a minute went by during all the remaining years of our marriage that I wasn't afraid of Greg falling apart again.

How can a woman remain in love with a man who could fall apart at any moment? How can a man remain in love with a woman who questions his every move?

When I was able to look past the anger I'd held for so many years, what I felt was an all-encompassing grief. I'd been robbed of Greg, too, and I had loved him once, the real Greg, the one underneath the illness. The moment had been brief, but it had unquestionably existed. Sometimes that fact was lost in the charade that became our marriage. Sometimes I forgot there had been a real Greg. It was no doubt easier that way. Anger motivates while grief incapacitates. I don't think I could have survived all those years if I'd allowed myself to grieve. The anger burned me alive, but at least it gave me the fuel I needed to make it from one day to the next.

Sick to death of my thoughts and unable to tear myself away from the memories, I plunged my hands into the icy creek and scrubbed my face with the freezing water. The shock was enough to banish Greg's ghost, at least for the time being. Returning to the boulder, I picked up the notebook and began to sketch my ideas.

Chapter 21: Sheriff John Moore

The best they could figure, it'd be at least a couple of days to get the car detailed. Mrs. Holt had done an excellent job of smearing mud from floorboard to ceiling, and that, combined with the soaking we'd given it, meant the upholstery was already beginning to take on a smell that can only be described as *wet dog*. I don't mind that smell, particularly (maybe because Roscoe, my golden retriever, smells that way often), but it seems most people do.

The car they'd gotten for me was an old beater, a good three years past its prime, the black paint oxidized and yellow trim cracking. I'd hoped for a shot at Cabell County's new Humvee, but as a smalltime sheriff in the middle of nowhere, that apparently wasn't going to happen. I grabbed a protein drink and, doing my best not to even dignify that pile of crap with a look, squeezed behind the wheel, whacking my bum knee on the steering column and letting loose a whole bunch of words I won't repeat. At least the storm had passed, which gave me some hope that Mrs. Holt might be clean and dry, for once. I hated to think what they'd give me to drive if she managed to trash that car, too. A bicycle, maybe? A mule?

I turned onto West Virginia Route 10, familiar enough with the old highway to make the trip with my eyes closed in spite of the potholes and switchbacks. In other places throughout the state sections of the old route were being rebuilt, but funding always seemed to run out before they got to our neck of the woods. To be honest, I was a little relieved. I liked it just the way it was: remote, unpopulated, forgotten. I didn't want the hassle of road equipment, and I sure as hell didn't want an improved system of roads to lead to an increase in population.

I'd always been a loner. Cedar Hollow and the surrounding area were perfect for me. The people were friendly, and if they had a natural inclination to be a little meddlesome, they at least responded well to my desire to be left alone. If I got lonely at times, well, that was better than the alternative.

To my way of thinking, Mrs. Holt and her problems were a perfect example of the alternative I wanted to avoid. Entanglements led to nowhere good, or at least that was my opinion, based on the experiences I'd had. I hadn't spoken to my mother or stepfather in years, and I didn't miss either one of them. Hell, for all I knew, they were dead. They'd been neglectful at best and abusive at worst, and once I'd escaped the nasty little roach-infested tract house they'd called home, I'd never gone back. My real father—meaning the man who'd fertilized the egg—had split before I was born. I had no idea who he even was, and to be honest, I didn't give a rat's ass. Or any other ass for that matter.

I'd had only one relationship that could rightly be classified as serious. That was with a woman I met in college shortly after returning to finish my degree, and that was enough to convince me I wasn't relationship material. She was beautiful, and I suppose I'd loved her. But I'd had a knack for upsetting her without having a clue what I'd done. I'd think everything was going along just fine, then all of a sudden she'd be crying and carrying on and accusing me of being distant, or uncaring, or secretive, or whatever-the-hell else. I didn't consider myself to be any of those things, but that difference of opinion didn't work very well to fix the problem, and one thing was certain: Whether I was or whether I wasn't, she was clearly miserable with me, and I couldn't stand myself for making someone else so miserable. I did us both a favor and left.

In the years since then, I'd come to a better understanding of myself, and I could see how in some ways she'd been right. It wasn't intentional, of course, but in hindsight, I can see how I might have come across as uncaring or secretive. I have always liked to go off by myself, camping, fishing, hiking, anywhere alone. That wasn't in any way supposed to indicate I didn't care about anyone; it's just what I needed to do. I need space to myself, always have. I'm not much of a talker, either. The truth of the matter is, I'm a simple man. If I have something to say, I say it. If there's something that needs doing, I do it. I accept things the way I see them. I'm not good at guessing what other people want from me, and that seems to be a serious shortfall when it comes to women. To most people in general, in fact.

I've given in to the occasional one-night stand in recent years, which is enough to meet my needs without getting me tangled up in something in which I already know I won't succeed. Apparently, the strong, silent type is perfect for a night or two, just not for much longer than that.

Emily Holt, though, seemed to me to be swallowed up by other people. She'd had a suicidal husband who'd accomplished his goal, and she had two grown kids who couldn't go a couple of weeks without her without feeling the need to call the police. That's about as tangled up as a person can get.

I thought back to that morning, her sliding down the mountain in the mud, trailing flowers behind her. Maybe she was a little crazy, but after learning more about her history, I had to admit, I felt a little sorry for her. Whatever it was she was doing in Cedar Hollow, it was pretty clear to me she wanted a break. It was also pretty clear she wasn't going to get one.

I took a right onto Deer Jump and slowed my speed. Deer Jump is such a narrow, winding road it makes Route 10 look like an interstate by comparison. Mrs. Holt had been lucky, not once, but twice, first because aside from the residents of Cedar Hollow, Deer Jump is largely untraveled, and second, because locals know how to drive these roads without acting like they're practicing for the Ona Speedway over by Huntington. The closest we'd had to a real accident in all the time I'd been patrolling the area was when a couple of teenaged boys ran off the road trying to get a good look at Geraldine Pritchett's granddaughter. They'd escaped serious injury and were still apparently too horny to even realize how close they'd come. "Who was that?" was the first thing they said when I pulled up to the scene. "She's *hot*!" was the second.

I was just about to turn left onto Main Street when I saw her walking down the side of the road, coming toward me. I almost didn't recognize her without the mud; both times I'd seen the woman she'd been soaked through. She was younger than I'd originally thought. Prettier, too. A whole lot prettier. She had a real healthy look about her, an outdoors look, if you know what I mean. A woman who appreciates being outside. Real natural.

Well, I'm not dead, after all.

I pulled up next to her and lowered the window. "Mrs. Holt? Do you have a minute?"

She stopped, apparently surprised to see me. "Nice ride," she said, looking straight at me and grinning. Most people don't make eye contact with me. It's something I've grown used to over the years. Hell, I'm not stupid. I know my size can be intimidating. From what I gather, I'm not approachable, either. That's not on purpose; it's just the way it is. But this woman, her grin was so unexpected I nearly grinned back before I caught myself.

"Well," I said, "as you can see, the county spares no expense. My other ride is temporarily out of commission, but I'd like to talk to you for a minute, if you don't mind. Seems you've got a couple of kids worried about you."

That got her attention. The grin left her face and she grabbed my arm, the one I had resting on the window. Her hands were cool against my skin. Cool, and soft.

Not that that meant anything to me. Because it didn't.

"What's wrong with them?" she asked, and I pulled my attention back to the job.

"Nothing, so far as I know. They're just worried about their mom. Were you headed back to Erma's? I'll give you a lift and tell you about it."

She nodded and rounded the front of the car as I leaned across to unlatch the passenger door. She slid in with a burst of cool air and the smell of the mountains, and I was reminded of my time in Morgantown. West Virginia University, the first time, before the busted knee, before the Marines and the nightmares, before the godawful engagement. I'd had big dreams back then, stupid little boy dreams that ended before they'd even begun. Why the smell of fresh air clinging to the half-crazy woman climbing into my car brought all that back, I couldn't have said.

Damn it all to hell.

Chapter 22: Zachary Holt

At first I thought I was camping, wrapped up too tight in my sleeping bag, sweaty and tangled and fighting to get out. Noah and I used to go camping with our scout troops when we were younger, and while the nights cooled off enough during the fall for us to comfortably use our sleeping bags, we were squirming and trying to get free of them as soon as the sun rose.

It wasn't until my struggling resulted in entrapment between the bed and the wall that I remembered where I was. Grabbing the outer edge of Noah's upper bunk, I managed to free myself from both sheets and blanket and haul myself onto the floor with a thud and what would undoubtedly turn out to be a bruised shoulder. How the hell we'd managed to spend so many years sleeping in bunk beds was beyond me. The bed in my dorm wasn't exactly big, but at least it wasn't enclosed. In the years I'd been gone, I seemed to have developed a healthy dose of claustrophobia when it came to my sleeping arrangements.

I stood, rubbing my shoulder, to see Noah was already up and gone, his bedcovers an even bigger mess than mine. Grabbing my phone from the windowsill I cursed, seeing I'd missed a call, one from an unfamiliar number. Apparently I'd forgotten to switch it from vibrate to ringtone before going to bed, a stupid mistake given our circumstances. I wasn't sure whether to be worried or relieved when I saw it wasn't my mother's number. I was glad I hadn't missed her call, but even more concerned we still hadn't heard from her.

I followed the smell of toaster pastries down the hallway and into the office, where I found Noah bent over Mom's desk, making notes in her appointment book. "I've already called the neighbors," he said. "She didn't say anything to them about leaving. Most of them didn't even notice she was gone. That's kind of sad, isn't it? Here," he said, handing me a saucer of pastries. "I'm not hungry. Any calls?" he asked, motioning toward my cell.

"Just some random number, a telemarketer or something."

He looked up from the desk. "Area code three-oh-four?" he asked. "I got the same call. Maybe we should—"

He was interrupted by the buzzing of his phone. "Orange Park Police Department," he said, checking the screen. "Zach?"

He looked at me, his eyes wide, and I had a sudden memory of him dangling from the lower branches of the Japanese plum tree in our backyard. He must have been around six years old at the time. We'd been practicing for a scout badge, and we'd gotten pretty good at climbing up. Our weakness was in climbing down. Our mother had placed a stepladder against the trunk to help us with that, but I'd taken advantage of her momentary absence to remove the ladder and dare Noah to jump.

Because I was older, and because he nearly always agreed to whatever crazy stunts I suggested, he'd taken me up on it. That is, until he'd straddled the limb and turned to see exactly how far away the ground was. The tree wasn't especially big; he probably wasn't over five feet up, but when you're only four-six, five feet can seem like a long way down. "Zach?" he'd asked then, just as he was asking now. With his feet swinging freely and his bluster gone, jumping seemed a much more dangerous prospect than it had from the ground. "I don't want to jump," he'd said, on the verge of tears. Back then, he'd been saved by our mother, who swatted me on the behind before reaching up to rescue Noah.

This time, he was on his own. We both were. What if the news on the other side of that phone call wasn't news we were prepared to hear? There wouldn't be anyone to catch either one of us; there was no one left.

The phone buzzed again while we looked at each other. "Better jump," I said, leaning against the desk for support.

Chapter 23: Emily Holt

We didn't celebrate our sixteenth anniversary with a date night, at least not the kind of date night one would typically expect. No, we spent our sixteenth anniversary in the emergency room, not because Greg exhibited signs of mania, and not because he'd sunken into a dangerous depression, but because he was exhibiting symptoms of what I suspected—and what was later confirmed—to be gonorrhea.

We filled his prescription, told the kids he had kidney stones, and I tucked him into bed with a bottle of Tylenol and the television remote. I took the kids, then ages eleven and thirteen, to the local arcade for pizza and games, relieved to be spending time with my boys instead of on an obligatory date with their father.

Greg and I had not been intimate in years by then. We'd tried, in the beginning, but we'd crossed a line that made it impossible. In many ways, our relationship had evolved into more of a parent/child relationship than a husband/wife one, a realization that didn't do much to spark desire.

I wasn't upset by Greg's infidelity, not only because we no longer had that sort of bond, but also because I knew it was just another tactic the illness used to destroy us. Greg never cheated on me when he was well, and I'm not sure *cheating* would be an accurate description for what he did when he wasn't. There was a point during Greg's manic episodes during which he felt invincible. He became insatiable. He stayed out all night, drank to excess, and went home with strangers. Sometimes he came home the next morning; sometimes he didn't.

On the few occasions the boys saw him come straggling in, I hustled him into the shower and complained loudly about his job, the long hours, the terrible deadlines that kept him up all night. If we were lucky, if there was an available bed and Greg met the specific criteria designated by law, he returned to inpatient treatment and the boys were told he'd had to travel again. If we weren't lucky, I planned events for the kids to keep them out of the house and kept my fingers crossed until we could get Greg admitted. Luckily—in spite of how often I use it, that word fairly reeks with irony—Greg was almost always absent during his bouts of mania, and when he was depressed he isolated, sitting alone in the dark, locking the door against all of us, making it easy to tell the boys he was working and couldn't be disturbed.

Greg's job was a much-needed stroke of luck in the darkness, although at the time he hadn't appreciated it for what it was. During the months of his initial breakdown, he lost most of his friends and all of his bandmates. I didn't fault them for leaving, though Greg certainly did. He felt betrayed, but I understood that although Greg's life had come to a screeching halt, theirs continued. They had to do what they had to do for themselves, their families, and their careers. They had no way of knowing when, or if, Greg would recover. By the time he did, they were long gone, playing their way without him through smoky bars all along the Rockies and beyond.

Those months were awful, not just emotionally, but financially. I tried to continue working, dragging the babies along with me for interviews, but after the third interview in which Noah spat-up and Zachary loudly announced he needed to go pee, I gave up. Who would hire a designer whose specialty was biofluids? Our parents were still working, and God knows I couldn't afford to hire a babysitter. Because we'd both been self-employed, we carried a private health insurance policy that wouldn't even come close to paying for

Greg's treatment; the stack of bills was accumulating on the kitchen counter, and my credit card had just been denied at our local grocery store.

I was the one who found the ad. I was scouring the *Gazette*, looking for work-at-home opportunities that held the slightest hint of legitimacy, when I saw it. It was placed by an entity called *Jingle House*, and I nearly passed over it, assuming it was for some sort of position in North Pole, Colorado, home of a Christmas-themed amusement park. I don't remember what made me take a second look. Maybe the word *composer* caught my eye. Whatever it was, I remain grateful to this day.

Jingle House was a warehouse of sorts for commercial ad music, the jingles accompanying commercials, those catchy little verses that stick with you and drive you nuts. It was a buyout deal; the composer composed for a steady paycheck and benefits, but sacrificed royalties because the company retained the copyright. Provided the applicant had a home studio, most of the work could be accomplished offsite.

It was perfect for Greg. Instead of the daily grind of office work, he'd have specific projects to complete. As long as the projects were submitted on time, the company didn't much care where Greg completed the work or how many hours he put in per day. The main office was in Jacksonville, Florida, and while some travel would be necessary, daily communications took place, when needed, via phone.

When he refused to apply, I applied for him. He was livid, feeling commercial jingles were below his level of talent. *Survival*, I yelled back at him, was a talent he needed to embrace, and fast, before we lost everything and ended up on the street. He couldn't stay with the kids, and I couldn't afford daycare. Jingle House it had to be.

The money was good, but I think what bothered Greg the most was the loss of copyright. "Don't you get it?" he asked more than once. "I could be earning on these until I die. But now they get to earn off of my work, because they have the copyright." I give myself credit that it wasn't until the hundredth or so time he complained that I pointed out to him he needed the structure. "Let's face it," I finally said. "You can't be self-employed. You can't regulate yourself. Give up the stupid copyright and just bring home a paycheck."

Some of the things I said to Greg over the years haunt me, but I couldn't see—and still can't—that I had any other choice.

He got the job and for nearly a year we made it work from Colorado, but even Greg could see the probability of that working long-term was slim. Flying was stressful for Greg, and stress was a trigger. It was only a matter of time until he either isolated in his Florida hotel room missing his meetings altogether, or did something embarrassing and potentially irreversible, resulting in the loss of his job. That's the thing about the illness. There were flashes of Greg, flashes of insight and accountability, lots of them. Many times, Greg was able to articulate what he needed, what could keep him stable. Other times the illness took over, misleading us both, a wolf in sheep's clothing, so to speak, and it was hard to know which time was which.

After that first year, we relocated to Jacksonville. The move was difficult for me. I hadn't wanted to leave my friends and family, and I disliked the climate intensely. I sobbed as I drove along I-75 behind Greg and the moving van, despairing at the ugly billboards littering the Georgia-Florida border. Triple X stores, boiled peanuts, and peaches, interspersed every so often with *Jesus Saves*. The extremes were depressing, as if porn and religion were engaged in a silent war beside the interstate. The ragged palms and sickly oaks along the flat, grey landscape looked nothing like the colorful brochures I'd studied.

"It's ugly," I told my mother during our first phone call after the move. I was alternately unpacking kitchen utensils, running after Zach, and checking on a sleeping Noah, all the while sweating profusely in spite of the rattling air-conditioning of the tiny apartment we first rented. "It's wet. And faded. And it looks like someone pissed over the entire state."

My mother laughed at my churlishness. "Give it time," she said. "You're not even giving it a chance." I eventually grew to appreciate the natural beauty of the area, but back then, I thought it was the most dreadful place I'd ever seen.

Within a year, we bought the home on Palmetto Street where we raised our boys, and we worked hard to quietly fit into the neighborhood. It was a nice home, nothing fancy, but certainly adequate. I may have even liked it under different circumstances. As things stood, it was little more than a prison to me.

These were the thoughts flying around my head as the sheriff dropped me back at Erma's. Before I could organize them, filing them into their appropriate places before calling my boys, Joseph met me at the door. "Just in time," he said. "You have a phone call."

I didn't know what I would say to them, how much I'd share, or what I could tell them regarding my future plans. I just had to trust we'd figure it all out eventually.

Chapter 24: Emily Holt

From insecurities to random thoughts, to bully issues and puberty, I'd always taught my boys to trust me. "There's nothing that should embarrass you," I'd said.

"I cleaned your cute little bottoms and wiped your messy little noses; you can't get much closer than that. Trust me with anything that worries you, anything you need to know." In hindsight, that probably went a long way toward explaining the awkwardness of our phone call. They'd been conditioned to trust me; I'd been conditioned to lie. Now I was forced to defend all the little—and not so little—lies that made up their childhood.

They were full of questions, and I did my best to answer them. Yes, sometimes—many times—the business trips were real, if there was an out-of-town client who insisted on meeting in person. Yes, their father really had been a musical genius; yes, the commendations and awards were legitimate. No, I hadn't known when we married, but neither had Greg. Yes, I had loved him. I didn't count that as an untruth, because I *had* loved him at one time. There were eight hospitalizations in all, three during one horrible year in which Greg's medications went haywire and stability was hard to hold onto.

"My senior year?" Zachary asked, no doubt remembering his father's absence from his high school graduation. Greg had been in the hospital at that time, of course. Otherwise, he'd never have missed such an important event. But that wasn't Greg's worst year, not by a longshot.

In fact, Greg had been stable for many months, nearly all of Zach's high school career, before sinking into a depression from which he'd never fully recovered. Greg blamed his job for sending him into that last spiral; he felt as if they were edging him out. Maybe he was right, although I never saw any proof of that. They'd known about Greg's diagnosis for a long time, by then. I'd had no choice but to tell them during one particularly bad period many years before. They were understanding, even kind. Greg was an asset to the company, they assured me, and I believed them. He had their full support. They'd been true to their word, at least as far as I could see, but Greg felt differently, and it's impossible to say who was right. If he'd had a contentious relationship with them toward the end, was it because they'd been looking for ways to cut ties with him, or was it because, in his paranoia, he'd created a contentious relationship?

I didn't share those details with my sons. There was nothing to be gained by bringing the boys into the darkness Greg felt at that time. "He was in the hospital during your graduation," I told Zach instead, "but that was the first time in years, and the last time he was ever admitted." It was true. Greg was never again admitted to the hospital, not because he didn't need it, but because he didn't meet the criteria for inpatient, at least not according to the admitting physician. Of course, now he was dead, so clearly the admitting physician had been wrong. Again, I chose not to share those particular details with the boys. What good could have possibly come from it?

I think the knowledge that Greg hadn't willingly missed his ceremony brought Zachary some comfort, albeit mixed with guilt, a feeling with which I was well acquainted. "I feel bad I was so angry," he said. "I just couldn't understand how he'd leave during my graduation. I wish I'd known. At least I'd have understood. I wouldn't have gotten mad at him."

"You may have understood," I said, "and you may not have. And you may still have been angry." I could certainly vouch for that. "I'm not convinced you knowing would have made it any easier. Look at your reaction now. Your first impulse is to blame yourself. Your father was ill, and you feel guilty. Would you have wanted twenty-one years of that?"

I knew my question was harsh, but I needed to make my point. Whatever Greg and I may have done wrong, I didn't think keeping the illness secret from our children fit into that category, not when they were younger. Better to believe yourself to have an aloof father than to blame yourself for having a father with a mental illness. Because that's what families tend to do. I've met enough of them throughout the years to know. They blame themselves. I didn't want that for my kids, and neither did Greg.

Off and on through the years, I'd joined support groups, weekly meetings of family members held in the basement of a local church. *Misery loves company*, I'd always heard, but the support groups always managed to prove that wrong. If I was miserable dealing with Greg's issues on my own, I was absolutely despairing by the end of those weekly meetings. Members ranged from young to old, from parents to children to spouses, and the tales they told did nothing to incite optimism. One evening, after an elderly woman had sobbed her way through the telling of her husband's latest hospitalization, I stood, clutching my purse. "I'm sorry," I said. "I'm sorry for you and your husband, and everyone here. But I can't do this. I need to believe there's some hope. I can't live with the idea that in forty years I could be you, sitting in that chair, telling those same stories. I'm sorry."

The group leader jogged after me as I strode to the door. "Every story is different," he said. "Every experience is different. You have to understand, the people who come here are nearly always the ones dealing with the most severe cases. They need the extra support that friends and families are often unable to give. That doesn't mean your experience will be the same as theirs. Please reconsider. *Your* story may be the very one to give *them* hope."

"I don't have any hope to give," I said, and I stepped out into the humid night.

That was a horrible year. Noah was in fifth grade, I remember, and Zach in seventh. Greg had been taking one particular medication for years without any evidence of negative side effects when he suddenly developed a series of uncontrollable tics and twitches, mainly in his face, but rapidly beginning to affect his arms. *Tardive dyskinesia*, they said, before trying him on anticonvulsants in an attempt to stop the tics. It didn't work, only made Greg sleep all the time, and he was becoming increasingly alarmed, as was I. The kids hadn't seemed to notice yet, but it was only a matter of time, and we both understood the possibility of the condition becoming permanent if something wasn't done to correct it.

Medication changes were always tough for Greg. Not only did he have to be weaned off the problematic medication, with all the resultant reemergence of symptoms, but we also had to wait weeks, even months, to determine the effectiveness of the new one. Sometimes the side effects outweighed the benefits. Sometimes the med just plain didn't work or even exacerbated his symptoms. It was hell; there's no other way to describe it.

It took the better part of a year and three hospitalizations for Greg to reach a consistent level of stability on the new meds. The boys only knew he traveled, and when he wasn't traveling, we were. After one horrible episode, I pulled them out of school and took them to the Everglades, a spur-of-the-moment trip conceived out of desperation. I suppose I should have been alarmed at my capacity to tell a believable lie, but there was no energy back then for self-doubt and recriminations. My job was to hold it all together, so that's what I did.

"Now what?" Noah was asking. "Are you coming home?" I could picture him on the extension in the office, one foot propped on the desk, the other nervously jiggling his leg. We still had a corded phone in the office, a staple of our hurricane emergency preparedness kit. Cell phones were useless without power, but corded phones remained functional, and Noah wouldn't mind being tethered to the desk. Zach, on the other hand, would have the cordless, pacing through the house as he talked. He had never liked to talk on the phone, and couldn't sit still while doing so. "Anything I need to say can be said by text," he'd once told me. Apparently he'd changed his mind for our current situation.

"Yeah," he chimed in. "When are you coming home?"

"Why don't you come here instead?" I hadn't known I was going to ask until I did, but it seemed to me to be the right solution. "We have a lot to talk about, and I think some of it may be easier here, away from everything." I hadn't thought of that previously, either, but once said, I knew it to be true. I scrambled to meet his—their—needs. "When are you finished with finals?"

"Well, that's a little up in the air, since we came rushing home to find you," said Zach, and I winced a little at his tone. When I'd heard both boys on the line, I'd realized my attempts to reach them had come too late. Not only had they worried at my absence, they'd also already discovered much of the information I'd meant to share. I felt terrible about both situations, and was grateful they seemed to be handling everything so well. I hadn't expected the phone call to be easy. I'd been quite lucky up until then, and most certainly deserved any anger Zach sent my way.

"I don't think we need to be too hard on Mom," Noah jumped in before I could respond. "She asked us to come home, remember? And we didn't. And I hadn't even noticed it'd been a couple of weeks since I'd heard from her until you mentioned it. Sorry, Mom," he added, "but it's true. You know how I lose track of time." I did; my younger son was very much like me in that regard. "Look, we'll figure it out and give you a call back, okay? I've already emailed my professors to see if I could do my exams online, since I didn't know how long it would take to find you." I felt another twinge of guilt, although I knew Noah hadn't intended any slight toward me.

"I'm here until at least Wednesday," I said, "since that's when my car will be ready. To be honest with you boys"—I drew a deep breath—"I'm not ready to come home." I waited, but there was silence on the other end. "I miss you both, and if coming here doesn't work for you, I'll obviously meet you wherever you want. But I'd really prefer it not be at home."

"Give us until tomorrow to figure out what to do," said Zach. "We can't just drop everything, you know."

"I know, Zach. And I'm sorry I didn't get in touch with you sooner. I did try, for what it's worth, but not until I'd already been gone a week. By then, I was in the mountains with such spotty reception I couldn't get a decent signal. You have to understand." I stopped. They had to understand what? I didn't understand it, myself; I certainly couldn't expect them to. "I don't know how to explain it," I said. "I just had to leave."

"We'll call you tomorrow," said Zach, and I heard the click as he disconnected.

"Mom?"

I felt a rush of relief at Noah's voice. "Yes, baby?"

"It'll be okay. Zach'll be okay. You know how he worries. He just, when we didn't know where you were, after Dad ... and then, with all the records we found ..."

"I know. You have every right to be upset, both because I left, and because we kept secrets from you. I can't imagine how the two of you must have felt, coming across those files. I hope someday you'll understand we did what we thought was best."

"I do," said Noah. "I think we both do. It's just a lot to take in, and we're both tired, and we've been so worried. We'll call you tomorrow, okay? So we can figure out what to do."

"Okay," I said. "I love you, Noah. Tell Zach I love him, too."

"We love you, too," he said, and ended the call.

I stood with the phone to my ear until the off-hook warning blared, startling me back to the present, and I returned the receiver to its cradle. I could hear my boarding home friends in the dining room, settling down to dinner. Hannah had delivered their food while I was on the phone, Erma pausing to squeeze my arm and mouth a "thank you" to me as she led Hannah to the table. I gazed toward the dining room, unsure of my next move. A part of me wanted to hide in my room. I was tired of having my raw emotions on display for everyone to see. Another part of me wanted to join my new friends, to glean comfort from their easy conversation and focus on something other than my own jumbled thoughts. I remained rooted to the spot, unable to decide, until I heard soft footsteps and looked up to see Geraldine Pritchett coming toward me from across the parlor.

She looked so fierce, with her dark eyes and sharp cheekbones, I was momentarily taken aback. I remembered her sharp questioning earlier that morning, how awkward I'd felt with the exchange. Had I done something wrong? Maybe Kay had been mistaken? Maybe Geraldine didn't like chicken and dumplings, after all. I'd buy her another dinner, or she could have mine, whatever I needed to do to fix the issue. But as she approached, I saw the severity of her expression had been a trick of the shadows; her eyes were sad, soulful in the late afternoon light. She stopped a few feet away from me.

"It's terrible, the way things can get so mixed up, ain't it?" she said quietly, reaching a bony hand to me, the veins nearly purple under the mottled skin. "But don't you give up, you hear? I did, once, when I shouldn't have. You make sure you don't." When I hesitated, she shook her hand, a nonverbal order for me to comply. "Come on, now. We're waitin' on you."

I took her hand and let her lead me to the dining room, oddly comforted by the strength of her grip.

Chapter 25: Emily Holt

I dreamt of Gregory again, but this time, it was different. This time, unlike the others, I didn't recognize it as a dream. It was real, as real as any Friday morning I've experienced over the past two decades of my life. I was shopping for groceries, something I've always hated doing, especially since the advent of superstores. It rankles me to have to walk what seems like a mile from the toothpaste to the meat counter, then another mile to the garden section. "Just think," I used to complain to my mother, "they could knock this whole place down and fill it instead with a row of specialty stores. A bakery here, fruits and vegetables next door, meat at the end. One small store for each section. It'd be so much nicer to shop that way, don't you think? If I have to hike, I'd rather do it outside."

"That's a lot like how it used to be," my mother had answered. "You went to the grocery store for groceries, and to the hardware store for hardware. The feed store carried feed, and the automotive store carried oil. Don't you remember? We used to go to the nursery for plants, and then stop by the bakery to get you and your father a donut. It's probably more convenient to have it all in one place, but I have to agree it takes the joy out of shopping."

In the dream, I was reliving that conversation with my mother, thinking of her—missing her—as I searched for bleach to aid me in my never-ending battle against mildew. I often did that, conversed with my mother in my mind, and my father too, depending on the scenario. I'd been alone, essentially, since my parents had passed away. I wasn't sure if those imaginary conversations kept me grounded, or if they were a harbinger of my own mental unraveling.

I also had a long history of repetitive dreams, dreams in which I was searching for something I could never find. It might be a person, a bathroom, or, as in this case, something as mundane as a jug of bleach. I didn't know what the dreams were supposed to signify. Maybe that something was missing in my life? Maybe that my life was nothing more than a repetition of routine acts? Well, duh. I didn't need a dream to tell me that.

At any rate, as I trekked down aisle after aisle, my flip-flops squeaking on the waxed tile, I summoned the presence of my mother as I did nearly every Friday morning at the superstore. *You'd think it'd be with the general cleansers*, I complained to her in my imaginary conversation, *but no, it's with the dish soap. What kind of sense does that make?*

Ah, there it was. I stooped, bending low to grab the handle, and then ...

"Now, that's a position I like." I heard the playful voice from behind me, and I froze. I was afraid to turn around. Greg was dead, after all, so how could he possibly be behind me, repeating the first words he'd ever spoken to me? *Mom? I asked my mother in my internal dialogue. Is that ...*

"And we thought I was the crazy one." Greg's mocking voice again. "Your mother says 'hello', by the way. She says to tell you to try vinegar and baking soda instead of bleach. Bleach will ruin the grout." My mother had chastised me about my overuse of bleach for years. I gently set the bottle back on the shelf and straightened, taking a moment to calm my nerves before turning to face whatever was behind me.

I was terrified, not because Greg had ever harmed me, but because I had harmed him. I suppose you could say I had killed him, although he was alone that night in the car. I'd had enough; I was leaving. The boys were both in college, Zach a junior and Noah a freshman. They'd made it; I'd done everything I was supposed to do to shield and protect them and it had worked. I was finished.

Greg had been in a years-long funk, ever since the hospitalization that kept him from Zach's graduation. I no longer remember the different combinations of meds, the many cocktails prescribed. I just knew they didn't work. I couldn't help him; I'd stopped trying ages ago. We barely spoke that last year, both of us existing in our own world of shadows, his created by faulty wiring, and mine created by my close proximity to him. I thought of Greg as a battery drain back then. His very presence sapped my energy and turned my world into shades of grey.

I hadn't formed a plan, plans never having been my strong suit. I'd had a vague awareness that the time was coming for me to leave, but I hadn't pinpointed a date or mapped an escape route. It was a Wednesday evening. I'd spent the afternoon doing yard work. It was a beautiful day, and I enjoyed being outside. For months, the planter on the north side had needed a handful of landscaping stones replaced, and I had nothing better to do with my time. Greg was home that day, holed up in the office. I'd heard him intermittently throughout the morning, arguing with someone, presumably by phone. I hadn't paid much attention to it, to be honest. To be even blunter, I'd gotten used to tuning him out. It was a matter of survival. To pay attention was to risk being sucked into the black hole that was Greg.

Before that time, if anyone had asked me which were worse, Greg's manic episodes or his depressed ones, I'd have said the mania, hands down. When Greg was caught in the upswing, he was unpredictable, grandiose and paranoid, even delusional. He engaged in behaviors that had the potential to hurt not only him, but others, as well. His depressions, on the other hand, were quiet by comparison. He isolated, holed up in the office. He could go days without really speaking to any of us. It wasn't pleasant, by any means, but it was a lot easier to hide than, say, Greg streaking naked through the backyard or rocking out at two in the morning. Until, that is, he spent months on end systematically sucking whatever little bits of joy I'd managed to preserve out of our home. I lived through that time feeling as if I were walking on quicksand; one wrong move and it would suck me under.

When I looked up from gardening to notice the sun sinking behind the house across the street, I realized not only had I skipped lunch, but I was also in danger of missing dinner if I didn't get a move on. I put up my tools, washed up at the spigot, and entered through the garage door, shucking my shoes on the welcome mat. Greg was pacing around the kitchen island, apparently waiting for me.

"I'm going to sue, Em," he said, never slowing his pace. "They're not going to get away with treating me like this."

I sighed, not bothering to hide my frustration. Greg was, in Greg's mind, continuously persecuted, whether by the mail carrier neglecting to latch the mailbox door, or because the car at the four-way stop stole his turn, everyone was always out to get Greg. It was exhausting. "Who, Greg?" I asked, turning my back to him and digging in the freezer for something quick and easy to cook. "Who are we suing this time?"

"Jingle House," he said, knocking a chair askew on his pass around the table. He didn't even pause. "They're cutting my hours. Giving my projects to some new kid. They've been trying to get rid of me for years."

I turned to face him. "Greg, do you think it's possible, just maybe, that they're giving your work away because you aren't getting it done? When's the last time you turned in a finished product?" I knew it was the wrong thing to say, but I was too tired to say the right one.

I don't remember all the things we yelled at one another, only that it was ugly. Sick of fighting, I went to bed, locking the door behind me, but Greg's pacing and muttering got me back up. I remember pulling my suitcase from the closet and packing. I remember Greg's accusations of infidelity. That was nothing new, but given his rounds of antibiotics and bouts with creepy crawlies, they were accusations that were especially hard to stomach. *Why the hell*, I remember thinking, *would I ever want another man? I can't even stand the one I have.*

I remember his threat to "just end it all, right here and now."

"Well, don't take me with you," I'd said, probably not the smartest response, but I was beyond caring. "I rather like it here." That statement wasn't even true; I'd just wanted to zing it at him.

His pacing had gotten more frantic. He knocked over a lamp and swept mail from the table, yelling about his keys, threatening to leave. Threatening to drive off the Fuller Warren Bridge.

"Go for it," I screamed at him. "You've been saying it for years; what's stopping you?" The bridge was Greg's ultimate threat. In his darkest moments, he'd hurl it at me out of desperation, as if it were a lifeline in reverse, something I could catch to haul him back in. It worked well in our earlier years. I'd beg and plead until Greg either fell asleep from exhaustion, or agreed to go for treatment. Over time, much like the parable of the boy who cried wolf, he'd worn out the power of that statement. I'd grown tired of reacting to a threat that never materialized. Greg always danced right up to the edge, but he'd never once gone over. That was the thing. That was what propelled me to respond as I did.

"I can't find my keys," he said softly, plaintively, and everything got quiet. He stopped pacing, standing completely still in front of me, shoulders hunched, arms dangling loosely by his sides.

"They're on the dresser." I made my voice as quiet as his. "Beside your wallet. Let me get them for you." I smirked when I returned to place the keys in his upturned hand. My face burns with shame at the memory. "Have a nice drive," I'd said, the last words I ever spoke to him.

He left, and I, with some relief, returned to bed. Two hours later, the Orange Park Police Department rang my doorbell. I was stunned. I hadn't really believed he'd do it. Had I?

All of this to say, I was afraid to turn and face the Greg-ghost behind me.

"I didn't do it, you know. Commit suicide."

My head snapped up at those words.

Greg laughed quietly, an amazing sound. I couldn't remember the last time I'd heard him laugh, and I'd forgotten how contagious it was. Greg had always had the kind of laugh that made people turn their heads to see what all the fun was about. People grinned without knowing why, moved by the sound of Greg's laugh. I turned to look at him.

What was behind me was Greg, but it was a version of Greg that very nearly took me to my knees. It wasn't the tired, wrecked, worn version I'd last seen, nor was it the banker-looking man from our wedding, or the drowning, Medusa-haired version from my dreams. No, this was the young, vibrant, *sexy* version I hadn't seen since—truthfully—before our marriage. He wore the same sleeveless t-shirt he'd worn on the day we met, the same ripped jeans, the same scuffed cowboy boots. And that *hair*. It was even more radiant than I'd remembered, hanging loosely down his back, the ends reaching just below the back pockets of his jeans, swinging out past his narrow hips. His eyes were bright and clear, and he was smiling at me, half-amused, I thought, and half-sad.

"How ironic, right?" he said. "I threaten to drive into the river for years, and the one night I decide *not* to do it, I end up killing myself."

"What are you talking about?" I could barely pull myself together enough to ask.

"I was coming home." He shifted his weight onto his right leg, hooking his thumbs into the outer corners of his front pockets. I'd loved that posture when we were dating. Daring, carefree, intriguing. Sensual as hell. All the things I'd believed we were. "I thought about the boys," he said, "and I couldn't do it. I knew, somehow, that I was being irrational. Remember how that used to happen?" He cocked his head, studying me. "I'd get these glimpses of myself and know I wasn't doing well."

I nodded. Greg had periodically had flashes of insight during the bad times, a parting of the mist in the middle of the storm. Not nearly often enough, but sometimes.

"It was one of those times," he was saying. "I was tired. I'd worn myself out, and I nodded off." He shrugged. "And that was that."

"I thought I killed you," I said. "I thought—"

"No," he said, shaking his head, making his hair fly out around him. "Come," he said. "Sit." He motioned to the bistro set behind him, his elegant fingers pointing, and I realized I was no longer in the superstore. The air was dark and hazy, tendrils of cigarette smoke drifting toward the ceiling. A single votive candle sat in an amber holder in the middle of the table, the flame flickering in an invisible breeze. Two drinks bracketed the candle, both in a Collins glass, both sweating on cocktail napkins, and I knew, beyond any doubt, they contained Jack and Coke, our favorite drink from days long gone.

The stage behind the table was bright with lighting, and Greg's equipment was piled along the back wall, waiting to be unpacked and hooked in. Vaguely, I was aware of voices, movement, the sound of laughter, the strains of a piped-in ballad sung by *Queen*, Freddie Mercury's tenor sliding up the scale with the ease of a *primo uomo*.

"You're young," I said, sitting awkwardly, uncomfortably aware that my backside spilled off the edges of the seat. In spite of everything, Greg's youth seemed to be what affected me the most. It stunned me, stopped me in my tracks, taking me to *before*. I could see our boys in his face, especially Zachary, who was close to the age Greg seemed to be. Had been, when we'd met. It was disconcerting, seeing the faces of my children in the face of the man with whom I'd once been in love. I'd never before noticed the resemblance, probably because the Greg I'd lived with was so far removed from the Greg I'd fallen for.

"I'm well," he countered, walking around the table to sit across from me.

"Does this mean I get to be young again, too?" I asked, a tentative smile playing at my lips. Whatever was happening, it wasn't the least bit frightening. To the contrary, there was something comforting about the experience. It was so familiar to me, invigorating, as if the past twenty-five years had only been a diversion, a momentary glance away. As if I'd found my lost love after a quarter of a century apart. I felt giddy, a feeling I hadn't had since those early days watching Greg and the band, when half-naked women threw scribbled phone numbers and lacy panties at their feet.

"It means you get to be well," he said. "Your most well self. This is mine. *Was* mine. Before everything happened. Do you remember?"

I nodded, my throat constricted by his words. I did remember, in spite of my best efforts to forget. "I don't want to remember," I finally managed to say, swiping at my face with my shirtsleeve.

Greg removed the damp cocktail napkin from under his glass and handed it to me. "I know," he said. "Neither did I. It's painful, isn't it?"

It was. I buried my face in the napkin, trying to regain my composure. Even admitting it was painful. I struggled to breathe.

"Easy, Em." Greg laid his hand on my arm, his long fingers gentle against my skin. My heart ached at the contact. I remembered that, too. Greg's touch. It was overwhelming. Heartbreaking, as if all the devastation, all the disappointment, all the wreckage of the last twenty-five years was wrapped into one unbearable moment.

"Greg, I—"

"We did okay, Em," he interrupted me. "We had two great kids, a decent home. Food on the table, as my dad used to say." He smiled, reaching over to grasp my hand with both of his. He was so warm, something else I'd forgotten. I don't know if his warmth left him over the years, or if I simply stopped getting close enough to feel it, but in the early days, I used to call Greg my personal space heater. I slept with my arms and legs wound around him on cold winter nights. How could I have forgotten these things?

"Who'd have ever thought I'd sound like my dad?" Greg continued. "But he had a point; we had all the essentials. Life handed us crap, but we made it work, didn't we? You have to look at it that way. You're a wonderful mother; you were a wonderful wife. You didn't give up on me. You didn't leave.

You toughed it out, in spite of everything." I opened my mouth to protest, but he shook his head. "No. You're the heroine in this story. You carried all of us. I'm just sorry you had to. If I could have changed it—"

It was my turn to interrupt him. "God, Greg, I'm so sorry." In an instant, the anger had melted, and I could see clearly for the first time in years. All I'd had, all I'd lost, all I'd managed to save. The grief I'd spent so many years trying to escape threatened to drown me.

"So am I," he said, "but it wasn't us. It wasn't our fault. We did the best we could."

"I should have—"

"No," he said. "It's not like it came with a manual. That's how I always thought of it, you know. When I was able to think, at least. As 'it'. Something apart from me. From us. It meant to destroy us, but it didn't. It only broke our hearts. We dealt with it the best we knew how. It beat us down," he said, "but it didn't win. Not unless you let it."

Greg's cocktail napkin had long since passed its usefulness; I'd resorted to my shirttail. This man in front of me, with the unbelievable hair and erotic hands, had been my first and only love, but I'd only been able to have him for such a short time.

"I love you, Em," he said, reaching to tilt my chin with his index finger.

"I love you, too, Greg," I said, and I did. I always had; I just hadn't always been able to find him.

"Tell the boys I love them," he said. "They're my heart and soul."

"I will," I said, with a catch in my voice. "I have to tell them, you know."

"I know," he said. "It's time."

"I'm not going to tell them everything," I said, squeezing Greg's hand. "And I'm going to lie about some things. I'm sorry if that makes me a terrible person."

"It makes you a compassionate person," he said. "They don't need to know everything. They only need to know enough. Thank you, Em." He leaned forward to kiss the hand he was holding, then scooted back in his chair.

"Do you have to leave?" I felt panicked at the thought.

He nodded toward the stage. "Time for our set," he said. "Gotta rock the house, girl. You know how it is." He smiled his crooked smile, his rocker smile, one corner quirked up, the other down. I would not have thought my heart capable of breaking, but it was. I felt it splintering into pieces, and I realized it hadn't broken before; it had frozen. It only broke with the melting.

"When will I see you again?" I couldn't help asking. I couldn't believe he'd appeared after all these years only to disappear again.

"Not for a long time. You've got a long way to go, girl. You haven't even begun to know your *well* self." He smiled at me. "You can't be it here until you've known it there. Now go and find it. Don't let the bastard win."

He leaned close to me over the table, and I closed my eyes for his kiss, a soft butterfly of a kiss that left me wanting more.

And then he was gone.

Chapter 26: Erma Puckett

The older I get, the less I sleep at night. Joseph says that's because I sneak a nap or two during the day, but I don't believe it. I'm not sleeping, I tell him. I'm just resting, leaning my head back for a quiet moment or two. "Resting," he says, teasing me, wiggling his eyebrows. "*Deeply* resting." He does make me smile, my Joseph.

I think maybe this old body doesn't want to sleep too much because it knows the eternal rest hovers somewhere just ahead of me. My spirit wants to enjoy every minute of this world while it still can. Either way, I've always been partial to the hour just before dawn. There's just something about it that feels fresh. Clean. The troubles of the day before are behind us, and the possibilities of a new day are ahead.

My mornings almost always start somewhere between four and five o'clock, when everyone else is still sleeping and I can greet the sunrise all by myself. I feel a little selfish about how much I enjoy that time to myself, but I also recognize no one else wants to get up early enough to enjoy it with me, so I suppose my little slice of selfishness is all right.

My routine—and I do love to have a routine—is to start the coffee percolating, step outside for my paper, and settle into the wingchair by the front window, the east-facing one looking over the street. I never turn my lamp on until my coffee is ready. No, I sit there and look out at the morning, still dark, still quiet, and still new. It's a glorious time, to tell you the truth. It's the last few moments that everything remains untouched, unspoiled by us with all our desires. I like to watch the sky start to lighten, waking up the birds for their morning songs.

When the coffee is ready, I get me a cup, turn on the lamp beside my chair, and look through the paper. I skip over all the articles about wars and murders and politics. I used to keep up with those, but I don't anymore. There doesn't seem to be much point; the wheels crank on whether or not I agree with the direction we're going. I also skip over the sales ads and coupons. If it's not in Mr. Smith's General Store, I likely don't need it, and Dennis Lane keeps his prices so reasonable I don't need a coupon to shop there. Same with the obituaries. If I knew the person, I already know they've passed on.

I give a quick once-over to local events, which aren't really local for Cedar Hollow; we don't have our own newspaper—unless you count the notices on Mr. Smith's bulletin board—and as small as we are, our local events are rarely ever carried in the city paper. I set aside the comics, and if it's a Sunday, the word puzzles, too, for Joseph. Then I turn to my favorite part: the advice columns. My word, some of the questions they get could make an old woman blush. Others could just about make you cry. There's so much tragedy in the world; I give thanks each and every day for the good fortune I've been blessed to have. Then there are the questions that are so silly they make you laugh, which is what I was doing when I heard Emily Holt coming down the stairs behind me.

"You're up early," I said, folding my paper closed and turning to greet her.

"I didn't see you there," she said, and I knew by her voice she was either coming down with a cold, or she'd been crying. My guess was the second one, but the light was too dim for me to be sure. I knew she'd had a phone call with her boys the evening before. She'd seemed a little unsettled by it. I wondered if that was what was bothering her.

"Just me and the birds," I said, waving her over to me. "We've made a habit of watching the sunrise together. You're welcome to join us. There's coffee in the kitchen, if you're in the mood for a cup."

"Thank you," she said, coming to curl up in a corner of the sofa, tucking her feet underneath a cushion. "I'll hold off on the coffee for now. I'm hoping to go back to sleep in a bit. I had a dream that woke me up."

I could see then that I'd been right. Her eyes were puffy. "Bad one?" I asked, not trying to get into her business, just letting her know she could talk about it if she wanted to.

"No. That's the funny thing. It was a happy one, the best I've ever had. But it left me lonely." She pulled the afghan from the back of the sofa and wrapped it around her shoulders. "It was about my husband. It didn't even seem like a dream; it was like he was really there, but not the way he was when he died, the way he was when we met." She sniffled. "Are you sure you have time for this? I didn't mean to interrupt you. You and the birds." She gave me a little smile, the tear-tracks on her cheeks shining in the lamplight.

I settled back in my chair. "All the time in the world," I said. "That sounds like quite a dream."

"Do you believe in ghosts?" she asked, hugging a throw pillow to her chest. "Because I think I just kissed one."

Now this could get interesting. I set my paper on the end table, allowing myself a brief moment in which to wonder what it would have been like to have an advice column. I bet Dear Abby never got asked anything like *that*. Some days, I thought I might have missed my calling.

"Tell me," I said, settling in.

Chapter 27: Noah Holt

Zach was having a hard time putting it all together in his head. He felt duped, I think, as if he'd been tricked by both Mom and Dad. I could see where he was coming from, but I thought he needed to cut them both some slack. Those are typical roles for me and Zach; he worries and makes a big deal out of things when I think he should just let it go.

"Would you have rather known?" I asked him. We had just hung up from our first conversation with Mom. I could tell he was upset during the phone call, and I thought he was being unfair to Mom. "Because I wouldn't have wanted to know," I said. "Look at it this way: Until today, wouldn't you have said we had a good childhood? Loving parents, stable home?" Zach nodded, so I continued. "Well, I don't think we'd have felt that way if, instead of thinking Mom surprised us with a trip to the Everglades, we'd known our dad was actually being carted off to the hospital in a straitjacket instead."

"I don't think he was—"

"I know, Zach. God, lighten up. But you get my point."

"Yeah, but you don't have to make it sound even worse than it was." He slumped to the floor, leaning back against the wall, propping his elbows on his knees. Neither of us had had enough sleep and we'd been hit with some pretty shocking stuff. All of which, instead of making me more understanding of Zach's position, just made me impatient with my brother.

"Well, how do you know he wasn't in a straitjacket?"

"I'm pretty sure that doesn't really happen," said Zach. "At least, not until you're already in the hospital. And besides, was there ever a time you thought Dad needed to be restrained?"

There wasn't. Lots of times he'd been absent, or he'd been—we thought—extremely busy and stressed with deadlines. Sometimes he'd get angry if we made too much noise, while other times he'd join in and play with us. We'd never known which would be his reaction; we'd relied on Mom to let us know. But he'd never, ever been violent or out of control, at least not that Zach or I had seen.

Which, I realized, could also have been a testament to how well Mom had protected us. Either way, for some reason none of that bothered me, maybe because I have a more laidback approach to life than Zach does. Like my Mom. Or at least, like my Mom used to be. That was the part that bothered me the most. And it made me kind of annoyed with Zach, to tell you the truth. We'd been shielded, but what about Mom? He seemed to keep forgetting about her in the equation. It had to have been hard for her, made even harder because she had to protect us.

"I'm just saying," Zach continued, "it would have been nice to know at some point. Like maybe when I left for college. I'm twenty-two years old, Noah. A grown man. I should have been told."

"Right," I said, "because you're handling it so well now. I'd have hated to see how you handled it just after leaving for college. You'd have probably quit and come right back home."

I couldn't help myself; Zach was annoying the hell out of me. Apparently he'd had enough of me, too, because we left each other alone for the rest of the evening, both of us texting and talking to professors, trying to get our schedules straightened out. It didn't feel as critical as it had before we'd known our mother was okay, but we seemed to have agreed without even talking about it that we were going to end up driving to West Virginia, and we had a lot to take care of before we could make that happen.

I was just clicking off from talking with Crusty Cortez (who turned out to be really nice, after all), when Zach came back to the office, handing me a peanut butter sandwich and a Coke. "Wednesday," he said, leaning against the doorframe. "Late. Sometime after nine o'clock. That's when I'll get back here. I managed to get all my exams crammed into three days, which should be fun." He pulled a face. "My last one is at ten o'clock Wednesday. I'll be done with it by noon, load up the car, and be home that night."

The fact that Zach had rearranged his schedule to get home sooner went a long way toward erasing my irritation with him, even more than did his offering of food. "I'll be here sometime Tuesday," I said. "I managed to rearrange a couple of exams times, but most of my professors haven't gotten back to me." That wasn't too surprising, since it was a weekend. "I'll leave messages telling them never mind, I got it figured out."

"I'll have to head out early tomorrow," said Zach. "Drive all day, then take my first exam at eight o'clock Monday morning. Doesn't leave much time for studying, does it?"

"Good thing you're smart," I said around a mouthful of sandwich. "I'm smarter, but you're up there, too."

Zach grinned. "Two words," he said. "ACT scores."

"I'm not sure 'ACT' counts as one word," I countered. "But if it does, two words right back at you. SAT scores."

We'd always been competitive, but for the majority of our lives, I got the short end of the stick. I was two years younger, after all. There wasn't much way for me to compete with him physically, at least not until my sophomore year in high school when I gained an inch on him. So I'd focused on academics, instead. For the most part, we'd been neck and neck. I hadn't quite caught up with him on the ACT, but I'd passed him on the SAT, college entrance exams that ultimately led to scholarships for both of us.

"Okay," said Zach, turning serious again. "When do you want to leave out? Thursday morning?"

Now that we knew Mom was okay and we had the entire summer in front of us, I didn't feel as rushed to get there. "How about Friday, instead?" I'd said. "That gives us Thursday to catch up on some sleep, get the house ready to leave, etcetera. How long are you wanting to stay?"

Zach shrugged. "I've got a few weeks before I have to go back." Zach was taking a couple of classes over the summer in order to graduate in August. "I think they start on the thirtieth, so I'm free until then."

"I don't start work until the twenty-seventh. Memorial Day." I'd volunteered for the shift. My family had never done much on Memorial Day, anyway, and with Dad gone, it just made more sense for me to spend the day bussing tables than to make someone else do it, someone who'd be missing out on their own family time. "Tell you what," I said, "why don't we pack enough for a couple of weeks and just see what happens? If we hate it, we'll come back early."

"Sounds good. It sounds like it's in the middle of nowhere, with no cell reception. I give it a couple of days, tops. Do you think Mom will come back with us?"

I shook my head. "I don't," I told him. "At least not right away."

Zach sighed. "If I'd had to guess we had a crazy member in our family, I would have put money on Mom." He turned, stretching his back. "Not bad crazy, just crazy," he said. "Listen, I have to get up early, so I'm going to bed soon. Do you mind if I take the top bunk this time? The bottom bunk is just too cramped for me."

I rubbed at the knot on top of my head, the one caused by my earlier collision with the popcorn ceiling. "Help yourself," I said. "It's nice and comfy."

"Thanks little brother," he said, on his way out the door.

"No, thank *you*," I said, and if he caught the mischievous note in my voice, he refrained from responding.

Chapter 28: Emily Holt

My boys were coming. Hour, hour-and-a-half, and they'd be pulling up to Erma's, at least if they'd stayed on schedule. I hadn't been able to speak with them since they'd crossed the state line and Zach had called from a gas station landline. "We've got to get a new carrier," he'd said. "If you're going to be spending time here, we've got to have a reliable way to communicate. This is ridiculous. I don't think they even make pay phones anymore, and I can't keep asking gas station attendants to use their phone. They look at me like I'm nuts."

"Well," I'd said, "it does run in the family, after all." I'd hoped my flippant comment would elicit a laugh, and it did. I'd been heartened by the conversation. In all the phone calls we'd had since the initial one the Saturday before, that was the first time Zach hadn't tried to talk me back home. He was always my prickly one, Zach was; he reminded me of his father in so many ways, a fact that used to keep me awake nights. I'd lie awake searching for signs that the anxiety had crossed over into paranoia, or the inherent introversion was turning into isolation, but those signs had never manifested, thank God. Instead, Zach seemed to have embodied the more sensitive side of his father's personality without the accompanying demons.

I'd chosen to spend my time waiting in the meadow. I'd spent a great deal of time there in the past few days. I'd completed sketches for Peggy's Diner and now we were just waiting for paints and materials to arrive. Kay was gathering old newspaper articles for matting and framing. A mine explosion back in the thirties that had been commemorated by a Hollywood movie, the return of a famous author; there was no shortage of articles, and I found myself amazed at the depth of life in a town that seemed so simple on the surface.

I was even more amazed at the stir my modest sketches had engendered. One afternoon at the diner, Valerie Poindexter had approached to request a meeting. "The whole library needs a facelift," she'd said, "but it's the children's area I'm particularly concerned with. It's in desperate need of an update and I'm afraid the trustees are terribly out of touch with what children are interested in these days. Is this something you'd be interested in taking on? And if it is, would Tuesday work for you? I'd like to show you around and also discuss your fee."

It was and it would. That conversation was quickly followed by one with Brother Hudson of the Cedar Hollow Baptist Church, whose main concern seemed to be the "just plain tackiness" of the church basement. "It's been the same since my grandfather pastored here," he said, "and that was back during the Great Depression, so you can imagine how dreadful it is. Dark, damp, and ... Well, I'll just show you, if you don't mind. Are you available on Wednesday? I'd need to meet fairly early, if you don't mind."

I hadn't minded, and I had ultimately agreed with him. The basement was all of the above: tacky, dark, and damp. It was going to take quite a bit of work to update the area, but I was not only up for the challenge, I looked forward to it.

I'd happily signed on for both projects, agreeing to accept a small sum for each, not much, but enough to cover my rent at Erma's for the time being. "Are you sure?" Valerie had asked. "That just doesn't seem like nearly enough. Why, if we called someone from the city to do this, we'd be out and arm and a leg."

I reassured her that the amount was more than adequate. "This is about much more than money, to me," I explained. "This is about finding my footing." She hadn't asked for an explanation, and I hadn't offered one. Instead, I'd agreed to return the following week with a rough draft.

I'd spent Tuesday afternoon and most of Wednesday perched happily on my boulder, sketching away, inspired by the beauty of the area. Light, breezy, encompassing the senses. I'd been trying to figure out how to incorporate elements of the meadow into the church basement when I'd been startled by a footstep behind me.

"Sorry," she said, as I turned. "I didn't mean to frighten you." I recognized the woman from the children's lodge; she'd been assisting kids at the diner. I have to admit, I was initially a little annoyed at the interruption, not only because I'd been deep in thought, working on my designs, but because ... well ... because it was *my* meadow. Who was this stranger invading my sanctuary?

"I'm Jessie," she said, extending a hand. "Jessica McIntosh." Jessica McIntosh? My eyes widened at the announcement.

The rich Jessie who owned the lodge, owned the mountain, the aid I'd seen who, cleaned up and glamorized, could be a dead-ringer for ... "Holy shit," I managed to say, and nearly fell off the boulder.

She smiled. "I don't often get that reaction out here," she said. "I'm just another aid, working with the kids. Mind if I sit?" She gestured toward the rock.

I *had* minded, but now that I knew who she was, I was awestruck. "What in the world are you doing *here*?" I asked, my manners shot to pieces. "I mean, it's a long way from Los Angeles."

"I grew up here," she said, scooting onto the boulder next to me. "This meadow, the creek, this boulder. I used to come here all the time. It was my sanctuary."

Holy shit, I nearly said again, but managed to restrain myself. "This boulder hides a little cave," she said, "up against the mountain. I used to hide in it, sometimes, when I was a little girl."

I couldn't resist; I slid down to crouch on the ground and take a look. "Well, I'll be," I said. There it was, a little underground cavern not five feet high, sloping back to maybe three feet, snuggled under the mountain.

"My mother discovered it before I did," she said. "I sneak out here whenever I get the chance, because it reminds me of her. But enough about me; what about you? What brings you to the sanctuary?" *The*, she'd said, not *my*. I don't know if I would have been as generous, allowing someone else to stake claim to my spot.

"It's beautiful," I said. "Peaceful. A good place to get my head together."

"It is that," she agreed. "The whole area is beautiful. If you go a little farther up, you'll come to the Rugged Creek Bridge, another peaceful spot, at least for another couple of months. By late May, early June, kids take over the creek, fishing, swimming. We take our residents fishing once a week during the summer months. They love it."

"How in the world did you decide to open a children's lodge?" I asked. "That's such a different lifestyle than I would have pictured for you."

"I made a promise to my mother." She shrugged. "And she made a promise to the nurse who looked after her in hospice. It's the best thing I've ever done, the cornerstone of my life. My mother absolutely loved this mountain. She lived on it for many years."

"Billy May," I said, the pieces coming together. "The one Corinne talks about. She was your mother."

"She was." Jessie smiled. "Still is. She's not gone just because she's dead, you know."

I laughed aloud. "You sound just like Corinne. She said something similar to me just the other day."

"Well, Corinne had a heavy influence in my raising, so it's no wonder I sound like her," said Jessie. "She's like a second mother to me. She's really quite a character."

"I can see that," I responded. "I've enjoyed getting to know her. How far away is the bridge you mentioned? I'd like to check it out sometime."

"Not far at all," Jessie said, pointing. "Just down the path a little ways. It's about to get crowded, though, any day now. Sheriff Moore is already patrolling the area."

"Patrolling? Why?" I couldn't imagine a reason for the sheriff to patrol such a lovely area.

"The kids," said Jessie. "Swimming is fine, fishing, too, but sometimes kids like to jump from the bridge. They're not supposed to; it's not safe. We all did it, though, during the spring melt, when the water was at its highest. Crazy." She shook her head. "It's a wonder we survived."

She looked out over the rushing creek. "Of course, not everyone did. Geraldine Pritchett—I'm assuming you've met her?" I nodded, picturing the fierce-looking woman from the boarding home. "Her son died jumping off the bridge. You can't see them now, because the water's high, but the bed is full of boulders. He was only thirteen years old, full of bravado, no doubt. And still, every year Sheriff Moore has to come out and lecture kids about jumping from the bridge."

I was so caught up in our conversation I'd barely noticed the chill settling over the meadow as the sun dropped below the mountaintop. There I'd been, nursing my wounds and feeling sorry for myself, and look at the blow life had dealt Geraldine Pritchett. I couldn't even imagine how a mother survived such a tragedy. "The stories here," I said, shaking my head. "I like to listen to Erma and Corinne, Kay, the people I've met since coming to town. I mean, I end up in this hidden little town by chance, a place you'd never think much of anything happens, and I hear the most incredible stories. Heartbreak, resiliency. It's just amazing."

She looked at me from her seat across the boulder. "You couldn't imagine," she said with a smile, "the secrets buried in Cedar Hollow. Now, it's getting late and it's going to get cold soon. I'm parked by the trail at the foot of the mountain. Do you need a ride?"

I didn't; I'd gotten my car back just that morning. She waved good-bye, then turned back, as if struck by a thought. "If you wouldn't mind," she said, "this is my safe place, too. My home. If you could just keep my presence here to yourself, I'd really appreciate it. These people"—she waved vaguely toward town—"are my friends and family. I really don't want anyone else, anyone from outside, to catch wind of it.

The last thing Cedar Hollow needs is paparazzi storming the town."

"Of course," I said. Truthfully, during our conversation I'd forgotten she wasn't just Jessie, a woman close to my own age who also appreciated the beauty of the area. She was Jessica McIntosh, famous Hollywood producer. "My lips are sealed; I won't mention it to a soul."

She waved and was gone. I hadn't seen her since then; for all I knew, she'd flown back to L.A. I'd been back to the meadow twice since then, for most of the day Thursday and again as I sat waiting for my boys.

I'd spent a great deal of time putting down my ideas for Valerie and Brother Hudson, but I wasn't always working. Sometimes, I just soaked in the sun and meditated. I'd walked to the bridge once, standing on it to gaze down at the roaring water beneath. The spring melt, Jessie had said, meaning kids would soon be congregating to dare each other to jump. I thought of Geraldine Pritchett and her son. I hadn't mentioned Jessie's disclosure to her, of course, but I looked at her differently. The severity of her expression stuck me as more sad than angry. The comments and questions I'd originally found harsh morphed into those of a woman whose energy was simply better spent making it from one day to the next buried under the burden she'd been assigned to carry.

I also spent time talking with Greg, as crazy as that may sound. He hadn't returned to my dreams; I didn't think he would. But I felt him, not his illness, but *him*, available whenever I needed him, and I'd needed him a great deal, faced with two boys eager for the truth. Thanks to those mental discussions with Greg, I had a proposition for Zachary and Noah.

I wasn't ready to return to the house on Palmetto Street. I didn't know if I would ever be. If Greg and I had moved our family to Florida under different circumstances, I may have felt differently, but as things were, I'd never been happy there. It wasn't just the struggles we'd had, or the memories I had, although that was certainly a part of it. My dislike was even more basic than that. I didn't like the climate. I hated the heat and humidity. I hated the bugs. I wasn't a strong swimmer and even had I been, I'd never have stepped foot into the ocean. Newscasters seemed to enjoy reminding people that our nearest beach was the shark capital of the U.S. Why would I want to get into the water, knowing that? Fresh water held even more dangers: snakes, alligators, and some sort of freaky amoeba that, if it found its way into your nose, could kill you.

I'd made the best of what, for me, had been a pretty miserable situation all the way around. I'd done it for the kids, and in spite of my bouts of anger, for Greg. But Greg was gone, and the boys would soon be leaving. I'd somehow gotten trapped into believing it was too late for me, but I'd realized those past few weeks it was never too late. Erma Puckett was in love at nearly ninety years of age; Geraldine Pritchett was building new relationships with her daughters after decades of no contact. Kay Langley was redecorating a diner that hadn't seen change in fifty years, and the mysterious Billy May had come back from the mountain, living the last thirty years of her life happy among the people of Cedar Hollow, raising a daughter who would not only one day be famous, but also kindhearted. If these women were any indication, I still had nearly half my life to live, and even if I didn't, I had now—this moment—and I needed to get to it.

I'd been torn, was still torn, between my own need to find some happiness, and my desire to protect the boys. But they were no longer boys. Zach would graduate at the end of the summer, and Noah would be a junior come fall. Neither of them had any idea where they'd end up. While they both enjoyed Florida, they also both knew they'd have to go where the jobs were, and there was just no way of knowing where that might be.

I would leave the house with them, if they agreed to my proposition. It was paid for, after all; there was no rush to sell it, and I wanted them to have that stability for as long as they considered Palmetto Street home. In my secret heart of hearts, I hoped they'd realize by the end of the summer that they, too, were ready to move on, and I could put it on the market. But if not, I'd hire a lawn service through fall and winter, and we'd take it one day at a time, for however long it took.

As for me, I'd stay in Cedar Hollow. I'd found everything for which I'd been longing. Mountains, friends, work. A home, at least for now. It had everything I needed at that precise moment in time. Erma had already agreed to rent the room to me for as long as I wanted it, and she'd floated an idea I accepted without hesitation: a sharply reduced rate for room and board in return for light housekeeping duties. "I don't know if you've noticed," she'd said with a smile, "but I'm getting on up in years. I've been planning to put a notice on the bulletin board at the store, looking for some part-time assistance, but if it's something you'd consider, I'd be much obliged to have your help." I accepted without qualms; it was the perfect arrangement.

Just as I hadn't known where the road would end, I didn't know how long I'd call Cedar Hollow home. Dennis Lane had already promised to repaint the number on the town's welcome sign, changing it from 219 to 220, a nice, even number. Would it stay that way? Well, that remained to be seen. And that was precisely the point.

Chapter 29: Noah Holt

"Geeze, Zach, slow down." He was scaring the crap out of me with the curves. The only curves we had to negotiate in Florida were either manmade in a lame attempt to make the neighborhood look more interesting, or long, slow curves taking us around lakes or retention ponds. Neither of those could compare to the kiss-your-ass-end curves we were flying around in West Virginia.

"Relax, little brother," he said. "Knoxville has mountains, remember? I got this." He had a point. If the speed with which he'd driven from Knoxville to Jacksonville Wednesday evening was any indication, he'd mastered the art of speeding around curves. I'd never been to Knoxville—home of the enemy—so I couldn't compare similarities. I just had to trust him.

It had been a strange week, beginning with our panicked trip home the Friday before to look for our mother, and ending with us taking a road trip to some little town in West Virginia no one's even heard of. I was looking forward to it. I'd never been to West Virginia. Heck, I'd hardly ever seen mountains, aside from those trips to visit family in Colorado. "But these are very different mountains, Noah," Mom had said during one of our phone calls. "Lush. Full of vegetation to the extent if there isn't a path, it's really hard to get around." I couldn't wait to try it. I'd done a little bit of rock climbing, first with scouts, and then with a club from school.

I knew it wasn't quite the same thing, but I thought it might help, and I was eager to put those skills to work.

If Zachary wasn't exactly excited by the trip, he was at least not as resentful as he'd initially seemed. In fact, we'd had a good time. He'd gotten home the night before and I'd had another frozen pizza waiting for him. He'd asked if that was all I knew how to cook. I'd told him it was either that, or cereal, then I'd thrown the potholder at him. He'd retaliated by throwing a roll of paper towels at me, and the fight was on. We'd torn apart the living room, overturning the couch and knocking a lamp from the table. It was just like old times, except without Mom there to yell at us to take it outside. I won two out three rounds. Zach said it was only because he was tired from driving, and then we straightened up the mess and made a list of things to get done the next day.

We'd mown the lawn, watered the plants, stopped the mail, cancelled the paper, and cleaned out the refrigerator. Zach worked on our laundry while I vacuumed and cleaned the bathrooms (I'd lost the coin toss). Then we rented a movie, bought a six pack of beer, and ordered Chinese. It was nice, being grownups in the house we'd grown up in.

We went to bed early, woke up at six, and were on the road by seven. We'd stopped only twice, once at the halfway point, five hours in, to fill up with gas and get something to eat. Once, before we even made it out of Jacksonville.

"We need to stop somewhere before we get on the interstate," I'd said to Zach as we buckled up and prepared to leave. "I need to get something."

"What?"

"A hat."

He looked sideways at me. "What kind of hat? We've got a whole rack of hats in the bedroom."

"A red one. Cowgirl. Don't ask."

"I'm asking, anyway," he said, his expression unreadable.

"I had a dream," I sighed. "Okay? About Dad. He told me we needed to stop and buy mom a red cowgirl hat." Zach sat in the driver's seat, turned toward me with his mouth hanging open. "Don't look at me like that. Just drive, okay? I'll run in and get it." There was a western store in Orange Park, quite close to our house.

"It's not that," Zach said, facing forward and turning the key. "It's just that I had the same dream."

"Get out," I said, turning to look at him as he backed the car down the driveway. "No way, man."

"No, I did. I dreamt we were loading up the car, just like we did this morning, and Dad was all of a sudden there, handing me stuff to put in the trunk. 'Don't forget to get your mother's hat,' he said. 'A red cowgirl hat. She's always wanted one.' He said it like you'd say, 'Don't forget to pick up the milk.' Like it was the most normal thing in the world to get."

Zach had a history of tricking me, like the time when I was seven and he told me Suzanne Frazier wanted me to hold her hand in the lunch line. She hadn't, not by a longshot. Or the time when I was ten and he woke me up in the early morning hours of a summer Saturday and convinced me I'd overslept on the first day of school. I hadn't realized he was lying until I'd showered and gone in search of breakfast, only to find my mother still sound asleep in bed. He'd felt pretty clever about that one. So it was possible he was lying, trying to trick me again, but his dream was so similar to the one I'd had, I was tempted to believe him. Besides, as long as we stopped and got the hat, it didn't matter.

We found the perfect one, red felt, and after some arguing, finally decided on a size. Zach has the biggest head—no surprise, there—so we guessed if it was about an inch too tight for me, it would probably fit Mom. She doesn't have a big head, but she has poufy hair; we had to take that into account. The sales clerk wrapped it in tissue paper and put it in a hatbox for us, one of those old-fashioned flowery boxes I knew my mom would love. We'd placed it on the backseat, where it sat just fine all the way through Georgia, South Carolina, North Carolina, and Virginia, right next to the box of my dad's medical records my mother had asked us to bring. "We'll burn them," she said, "because that's not who he was."

But shortly after we'd exited I-64 West and wound our way to Deer Jump, a narrow, winding road that could best be described as a paved pathway, the hatbox slid off during one of Zach's crazy curves. I had just reached behind me, trying to find it without removing my seatbelt, when we were jolted to the side with a *bang*.

"What the heck?" I asked, while Zach fought with the steering wheel.

"Blowout," he said. "Dammit." He managed to straighten the car, pulling it over to the side, where it still remained half-on, half-off the road, right in the middle of a bend. "What now? There's nowhere to pull over."

He was right. My door was nearly touching the side of the rock wall of mountain, while the opposite shoulder dropped off what looked to be a sheer cliff. "I have no idea. We'll get killed, trying to change a tire out there. Which tire is it, anyway?" I asked. I hadn't been able to tell.

"Back passenger, I think. My cell's got no signal at all. How about yours?"

I checked. "Nope. Not even a bar."

"Worst case scenario is we walk," he said. "We're almost there, if the directions are right. I just hate to leave my car here. It's bound to get hit, and I don't want anyone getting hurt." He drummed his thumbs on the steering wheel for a moment. "Let's have a look," he said, opening his door a crack. "We can't stay here. Might as well see what the damage is so we can get some help when we get to town. Just stay out of the road. As much as you can, at least."

There wasn't room for me to squeeze out through my car door; I had to wait for Zach to turn on the hazards and exit his side before crawling across the console to follow him. We'd just rounded the back of the car and squatted down to take a look when we heard the blip of a siren. I stood, but Zach, who'd been crouched leaning forward, lost his balance and fell face-first in the dirt.

Lights flashing, the sheriff's car pulled up behind us as I reached down to help Zach. A huge man absolutely stacked with muscle unfolded himself from inside, replacing his hat on his head and closing the door before slowly walking toward us, the crunch of each step extra-loud in the quiet of the country road. Zach managed to right himself and gain his feet, brushing gravel from his front as he stood next to me.

The sheriff didn't say anything for a minute, just stood with his hands on his hips, looking at us, sort of bouncing on his toes. Then he gave this big sigh, the kind my mother used to give when we'd worn her patience to an end. Zach and I looked at each other, and I had an almost overwhelming urge to grab his hand, something I hadn't done since kindergarten.

What had we done? For Pete's sake, it wasn't *our* fault we'd had a flat. Maybe they should pave the stupid roads more than once a century, and create a damn shoulder, while they're at it. Then another thought hit me: *We're alone on a backwoods country road with a psycho cop.* That wasn't a pleasant thought at all, let me tell you. The movie *Deliverance*, anyone? Remember? I sure did.

"Let me guess," the man finally said, tilting his head back and switching a toothpick from one side of his mouth to the other. "You boys belong to Emily Holt."

Chapter 30: Kay Langley

Peggy's Diner was hopping that night, even more than usual for a Friday night. It could have been because Friday night was catfish night, with the thick, flavorful fish fried up in my momma's batter and her hushpuppies nestled alongside with a cup of coleslaw. That was one of our very best meals, always had been, so long as I could keep Andrew's heavy hand away from the pepper. Or it could have been because Riva and I are such good company people want to spend their Friday evenings with us. After all, Riva'd come back sporting hair just a shade blonder than it'd been when she'd made her last trip to the Huntington mall, and I was wearing my purple blouse, which, Hannah's opinion aside, I thought was quite nice.

Or, it could have been because Geraldine Pritchett's granddaughter, Marissa Sloan, was in town, bared bellybutton and all, coming to spend her last summer before college with her grandmother. Marissa, sweet girl though she is, always does cause a stir among the young men of Cedar Hollow. Some of the older ones, too, I'm willing to bet and sorry to say. She is a beauty, that girl.

It could have been all those things, and likely was. But it was more than that, too. I 'spect a part of it had to do with the easel Riva had put up front, the one with Emily Holt's drawings. People had heard the diner was going to get a remodel, and they were both curious and eager to voice their opinions. We are a bunch of opinionated folk, after all.

Then, too, it could have had to do with the red cowgirl hat hanging on the hook by the door, put there by Emily Holt when she came in with her shiny red cowgirl boots, wildflowers tucked into her hair, looking for a table. Another part of it likely had to do with those two big strapping sons she brought in with her. I shooed Hannah away more than once when she stood staring at them, and I hadn't missed the looks Marissa Sloan had been giving them, either. Lord have mercy, hormones were running amuck in my diner that night, there ain't no doubt about that, and I was plumb exhausted at the thought of it all.

The boys were every bit as handsome as Valerie had said they were; I'll give them that. She first caught sight of them when Sheriff Moore pulled into town, followed by Clifford and Maxwell Hager towing yet another strange car back to the repair shop. Said he'd had one boy in the front and another in the back when he pulled up to Erma's and Emily came running outside to meet them. Said the taller one hugged his momma, then reached back into Sheriff Moore's car for a hatbox. Said as soon as Emily opened it, she burst into tears, jumping up and down and squealing like a young girl.

At this part, Corinne Johnson broke into the conversation, from where she'd been sitting at a front table with a glass of iced tea. "I *told* Emily it looked to me like she was goin' through the change," she said. "All that cryin' and whatnot. I'll have to remind Erma about the licorice." Riva and I just looked at each other; didn't neither one of us know what Corinne was talking about, but I considered it more proof of what I'd said: Hormones were running amuck in my diner that night, and from both ends of the spectrum, if what Corinne said had any truth to it.

Looked like the Holt family was going to be staying with us for a while, and I was glad to hear it. That woman had brought some sort of energy into town, livened things up a little, shaken us all out of our habits. It's good to be shaken up a little every once in a while; it gets the blood moving again. And it's without a doubt good for business, which was mighty helpful given the project we'd just taken on.

I handed Hanna a tray of steaming catfish plates and pushed her forward, in the opposite direction from the Holt brothers. Lord, that child. You'd think these girls had never seen a boy before.

"Did you hear about the sheriff?" Riva came up behind me, whispering in my ear.

"What?" I asked, turning to her. "That he found the boys in the middle of the road?"

"No," she said, leaning forward so no one else could hear. "That he *smiled*. When Emily Holt put on the cowgirl hat, dancin' around and squealin' like she did, he *smiled*."

Now *that* was newsworthy, no doubt about it.

Just then, Dennis Lane came through the door, holding it for his father, Darryl, and dropped some papers onto a pile on the counter. Copies of the original blueprints for Mr. Smith's General Store, I knew, found in a box hidden under the rafters. And on my counter underneath those, a moonshine recipe from Geraldine Pritchett. "Junior would kill me," she'd said, "but then, he nearly did, a time or two."

Underneath the recipe was an old paystub donated by Virgil Young, from shaft number twenty-seven, the mine that exploded and killed so many of our men back in the thirties. Finally, there was stack of library cards from when old Ms. Temple ruled the library with an iron hand and a kind heart. Back in the back, already framed and waiting for opening day, was an original menu from the first year of Peggy's Diner, when Peggy was still a toddler and her father, my grandfather, moved past the heartache of losing his sons and named the place after her.

We'd put out the word, Riva and me had, that the diner represented all of us, the whole town, and people had responded, bringing us recipes, photos, and copies of old family documents. Each and every one of them would be carefully framed in a red wooden frame and hung on the wall. The diner was for all of us; it was only fair it reflected that fact.

What no one knew yet was that I'd called the Barrett family, the descendants of the man who'd originally owned the land that later became Cedar Hollow. William Barrett was buried in the Cedar Hollow Baptist Church cemetery—was the first to be buried there, in fact—in 1831. His descendants had recently visited Cedar Hollow. They were a delightful family, and they'd agreed to send copies of the documents outlining the history of the land, from King George III, to the Savage Land Grant, to William Barrett, to the town of Cedar Hollow.

Riva had suggested a party to celebrate Peggy's Diner when the remodel was done, but I'd originally declined, not wanting to make a fuss. The more I thought of it, though, the more I liked the idea. Why not? As I looked over my diner that night, I felt love for each and every person in it. We were a town, but we were more than that. We were a family, too. Nothing, to my way of thinking, is worth celebrating more than that.

Chapter 31: Sheriff John Moore

I make my last loop of the night, just like I always do, making sure the residents of Cedar Hollow are safe before heading home to Roscoe. He's a good dog, able to care for himself for the most part on days I get home later than normal. He has a dog-door and a fenced-in backyard, but I still feel guilty when I leave him alone for too long.

I take my job seriously; I feel personally responsible for the people in my area. It's for that reason, and that reason only, that I decide to stop by the diner before going home. We've had a lot of strange happenings lately, unknown people showing up in town, getting people all riled up. It seems to me the Holt woman has her hands in everything, redoing the diner, the library, even the church basement.

Who does she think she is, coming into my town and butting in that way? I can't see what it is everyone likes so much about her, anyway. She's flat-out crazy, is what she is. Best to keep an eye on her, make sure she's on the up and up. That is my job, after all.

Besides, a man's got to eat. I'll pick up some catfish to go and while I'm there, see if Andrew has any meat scraps for Roscoe. He's partial to roast beef. Roscoe, I mean. I don't know about Andrew.

The parking lot is absolutely packed. I find a spot by the road and exit my car, standing for a minute, surveying the crowd. I can see Andrew's wife, Teresa, through the front window. She's cleaning off a table in the back, their youngest strapped into one of those harness things parents sometimes wear. Apparently, the crowd is more than Kay and Riva can handle by themselves, even with that little girl—I believe her name is Hannah—running around giving drink refills. They'd had to call in Teresa, baby and all.

Just one more way the Holt woman is putting a kink into things.

The Sloan girl is visiting, I see, sitting with her grandmother but making eyes at the younger of the two Holt brothers. He's looking right back at her, too, giving her a little nod. I know that look. That's the look boys have right before they run into the ditch because they haven't kept their eyes—and mind—on the road. More potential trouble; more to keep an eye on.

Emily Holt, dressed in a bright red blouse, is sitting between the boys and talking a mile a minute, using her hands to describe something. The memory of her cool hand on my arm flashes behind my eyes, but I file it away. Of course the woman has cool hands; she's forever rolling around in the mud. Crazy as a loon, that one. Her hair is piled on top of her head the way some women do, some curly parts of it hanging down by her face, and she's got flowers tucked into it. Real ones, from what I can tell. Her cheeks are flushed pink, as if she's excited, or maybe just happy. The smell of the mountains, I remember, but of course that's to be expected if a woman sticks weeds in her hair.

While I watch, she smiles at her older boy and he leans over to give her a hug around the shoulders. The younger boy manages to tear his attention away from Geraldine's granddaughter long enough to lean over and hug his mother's other side. All three of them sit there for a minute, holding onto each other. I look away; it doesn't seem right to stare.

The evening is growing cooler, taking me back to my old football days the way cool evenings always do. The excitement in the air before a game, the anticipation, the challenge; I could feel it in the air like electricity back then, sending charges up my spine, prickling my scalp. I missed that feeling when it was over. I haven't felt anything quite like it since. Odd, though, I could swear I get a whiff of it tonight, standing outside Peggy's Diner. My senses are on high alert, my scalp prickling, my heart rate increasing. Must be a storm coming; that's the only way to explain it. I turn back to the diner.

Teresa has finished cleaning off the back table, taking the blue tub and walking back to the kitchen area. If I hurry, I can probably beat the young couple pulling into the lot and claim it for myself. Roscoe will be fine for another hour, especially if Andrew has some roast beef scraps for him. Besides, I can monitor things better from inside. Make sure everyone is safe. Keep an eye on Emily Holt.

That is my job, after all.

Shadow Days Book Club Discussion Starters

In what way is the title a metaphor for this novel? Is it accurate?

When speaking of a "bucket list," Emily says, "...the big things on the list, things like *Live in a Monastery for A Week* and *Go on Safari in Africa*, seemed easier to me to complete than the little things, things like *Wear a Beret to the PTA Meeting* and *Stand Up to Your Mother-in-Law*. Do you agree? Why or why not?

Zachary tells his brother, "... it would have been nice to know at some point. Like maybe when I left for college. I'm twenty-two years old, Noah. A grown man. I should have been told." Do you agree? Should Greg and Emily have been more honest with their children? If so, when?

Unlike Zachary, Noah is glad not to have known the truth about his father's illness. "Look at it this way," he told Zach. "Until today, wouldn't you have said we had a good childhood? Loving parents, stable home?" Zach nodded, so he continued. "Well, I don't think we'd have felt that way if, instead of thinking Mom surprised us with a trip to the Everglades, we'd known our dad was actually being carted off to the hospital in a straitjacket instead." What do you think about Noah's assessment? Would knowing the real reason for the trip have negated the happy memories Noah has?

Regarding Greg's accident, Emily says, "I suppose you could say I had killed him, although he was alone that night in the car." Greg later explains that the accident was unintentional, but is it still possible Emily holds some responsibility for Greg's death? Why or why not?

Greg says, "It's not like it came with a manual. That's how I always thought of it, you know. When I was able to think, at least. As 'it'. Something apart from me. From us. It meant to destroy us, but it didn't. It only broke our hearts." What do you think of Greg's conceptualization of his illness? What might be the benefits of recognizing the illness as something separate and apart from himself?

Emily says, "I didn't start crying until I saw the old woman bent over a claw-foot tub shaking bath salts into steaming water." Why might this have caused Emily to cry?

When speaking of regret, Corinne says, "... it seems to me if you've done somethin' you regret, somethin' that changed the whole course of a life, either yours or someone you loved, you wouldn't want to forget it, not completely. You'd want to remember it so you don't never do it again." Do you agree with this view? Why or why not?

When speaking of Greg's paranoia, Emily says, "The sad irony of Greg's life: He reacted in such a way to his delusions that they eventually became real." What does she mean by this?

Was Emily's initial anger toward Greg justified? Why or why not?

A Note from the Author

A couple of years ago my family members and I collaborated on a series of short stories about the residents of the fictional town of Cedar Hollow, West Virginia. My previous publisher released the stories under the title *Cedar Hollow Anthology*, and proceeds from the book went to benefit my younger brother's adult developmental center. I left my publisher in 2013, and because the fundraiser had met its goal, the anthology was retired.

Since that time, I've re-released several of the stories under the series title *Snippets from Cedar Hollow*. Details from several of those short stories resurfaced in *Shadow Days*. As mentioned previously, Sheriff John Moore's character was explored by W. Michael Franklin in his short story, "The Sheriff of Cedar Hollow." Erma Puckett's character, including her relationship with Joseph Ammons, was more clearly developed in the Pushcart Prize-nominated short story, "Erma Puckett's Moment of Indiscretion." The Barrett family, mentioned by Kay Langley in Chapter 30, was first introduced in the short story, "A Treasure Box Full of Cedar Hollow." Darryl Lane, elderly father of Dennis Lane, the current owner of Mr. Smith's General Store, is the focal character in the short story, "Goin' Fishin'."

I anticipate releasing more *Snippets from Cedar Hollow* in the future, but felt the following story, "Spirit of the Mountain," simply had to be included in the back of this novel. Slight modifications have been made since the original story was published, but only because there are now more people in Cedar Hollow for Billy May to look after. The memory of Billy May was so strong in this novel, it seemed only fitting she end the story.

Spirit of the Mountain: A Word from Billy May

It is the time of *nvda gahlvsga*, the plantin' moon, as my Cherokee momma would have said. She let most of the old language go after she met my daddy, but I managed to keep some of her native words with me. I always thought my momma's words was beautiful, but I reckon she didn't have no one to speak 'em to after she left her people to be with us. My momma was a lonesome woman for the last years she was here upon this earth, but she's all right now, she is.

Contrary to my momma, my daddy held fierce to his native language, as if he thought by holdin' on he could keep a little piece of Ireland in his hands. *Féach ar an ghealach, Billy May*, he would say to me tonight. *Look at the moon.*

The moon hangin' over Cedar Hollow tonight is bright, though it ain't full. Still, the light shinin' down over the little town gives it a soft look, and I feel a tug at my heart from the sight of it. I had a good life here, and that is the truth. I have been a very blessed woman.

I don't come here as much as I did in the beginnin'. As Polly, the woman who took care of me, used to say, "There is a time and place for everythin'." I do believe she was right. For a while after I passed, this here mountain continued to be my time and place. My spirit wouldn't leave it, no matter how much my loved ones on the other side called out to me. I suppose that's because my heart and soul are so much a part of these mountains it's right hard to separate everythin' out.

In the woods behind me an owl makes his soft call, and somethin' rustles through the vines at the sound of it. The air against my face is cool and damp and carries the scent of mushrooms and crushed leaves. Across from my little cabin, the children's lodge that Jessie built is settlin' down for the night.

The lights go off, one by one, until all that's left is a glow in the far end where the office is. I know that Jessie herself has tucked little Robby O'Brien in for the night, kissin' his forehead and smoothin' his hair back just like I used to do hers (and still do, truth be told, if her heart calls out for me). Some nights, Robby tosses and turns with the worries, but this won't be one of those nights. He'll sleep peaceful tonight with Jessie there, knowin' his momma is comin' to get him in the mornin'.

I know that Jessie will visit with Richard and Opal Huffman in their suite before she goes to her own room for her nightly phone call with Michael, the man I wish I could have met and am glad Jessie finally did. My little girl is goin' to be just fine. She has people who love her, on her side and mine, and we're all watchin' out for her, believe you me.

I know that down in the town, Dennis and Darryl Lane are sittin' at the counter of Peggy's Diner, eatin' a piece of pie while they visit with Kay. I know that Mary Young's follow-up test came back clear, and she and Virgil are celebratin' by holdin' each other on the porch swing and lookin' at the same moon that floats above me. I know that Erma Puckett is up late at the boardin' home playin' cards with Geraldine Pritchett and a man who, givin' the blush on Erma's cheeks, is someone from the past—someone *important*, I'd say.

Clifford and Maxwell Hager are at the machine shop their daddy bought from Corinne Johnson after John Paul died. They're changin' a tire for Dr. Poindexter before closin' up for the night. Dr. Poindexter's wife Valerie, the librarian that lent me *Jonathan Livingston Seagull* all them years ago, bless her heart, is teasin' her husband, sayin', "It's a good thing you're better at fixing teeth than you are at fixing cars."

There's a new family as I look over the town tonight. They're sittin' on Erma's front step, a momma and her two boys, and the love surroundin' their little family brings a smile to my face. They're excited about somethin', lookin' toward the future with clear eyes and happy hearts.

Sheriff Moore slows and waves on his way out of town, and I feel the lightness in his spirit. I know that he has had good news today, and I know that he's been thinkin' about goin' fishin' on his next day off, maybe even callin' an old football friend to go with him. He puts the window down and turns the radio up; strains of Billy Joel's *An Innocent Man* float through the night and are heard by Corinne Johnson, where she stands in the darkness of her yard, gazin' up at Crutcher Mountain.

The breeze is blowin' a strand of her silver hair loose from its clip and she reaches up to tuck it behind her ear just like she's been doin' all her life. Her housecoat flaps around her legs and she crosses her arms over her chest, pullin' the collar close. She is still beautiful, after all these years. She breathes deep and sighs, and I know she's smellin' the same mountain scents I am.

I do not remember a time when I did not love Corinne. I whisper the words on the wind, and she smiles at the night, and at me.

Tá sé am chun dul, my daddy whispers to me. *It's time to go, Billy May*. And it is. But I'll be back if ever they need me.

You can count on that.

More Books by Melinda Clayton

Appalachian Justice, Cedar Hollow Series, Book 1

Return to Crutcher Mountain, Cedar Hollow Series, Book 2

Entangled Thorns, Cedar Hollow Series, Book 3

Blessed Are the Wholly Broken

A Woman Misunderstood

Child of Sorrow

Making Amends

About the Author

Melinda Clayton has published numerous articles and short stories in various print and online magazines. In addition to writing, she has an Ed.D. in Education Administration, is a licensed psychotherapist in the states of Florida and Colorado (on retired status), is a writing tutor, and teaches for Southern New Hampshire University's COCE MFA program.